The Absent Traveler:
A Novella & Other
Stories

RANDALL DEVALLANCE

THE ABSENT TRAVELER

A NOVELLA & OTHER STORIES

An Atticus Trade Paperback Original
Atticus Books LLC
3766 Howard Avenue, Suite 202
Kensington MD 20895
http://atticusbooksonline.com

"Decline and Fall" (2006) and "The" (2004) originally appeared on the
literary website, Eyeshot (http://eyeshot.net)

ISBN-13: 978-0-9845105-2-8
ISBN-10: 0-9845105-2-4

Cover design by Anton Khodakovsky

To Laura -

Fear not that thy life shall come to an end, but rather fear that it shall have a beginning.*

*adapted from John Henry Cardinal Newman

TABLE OF CONTENTS

Novella

Novella

The Absent Traveler

Jasmine had called. She wanted to see Charles, told him she missed him. She hadn't bothered to call him six years ago, when she packed up her stuff and disappeared late one summer's evening, but now she was back, like some old photograph dug out from under the clutter of life's passage. Like nothing had ever changed.

"Charles Lime?" she said, when he picked up the phone.

"This is he," said Charles.

"Guess who!"

He didn't have to guess. Jasmine had one of those voices that burned itself into your memory. Not that it was particularly high-pitched or deep or soft or loud, but it was hers and hers alone. It surprised him so much to hear her that he almost dropped the phone, and it was a few seconds before he could think of anything to say.

She laughed, like she'd been expecting something of the sort to happen. He finally managed to ask her what she was up to, and she said she was back in town taking care of her aunt, Eleanor.

"Auntie's not feeling well," she said. Did Charles want to get together with her that evening to talk? He said he did.

They planned to meet at the Café Lisbon for drinks at seven.

It was a quarter till when Charles arrived. The place was small and dimly lit, the walls plastered with colorful Moroccan tiles, and everywhere one looked—along the bar and on the tables and decorative shelves scattered throughout the room—were tiny frog figurines. Charles liked it right away.

Jasmine was already there waiting for him, seated in a booth along the wall. When she caught sight of him coming toward her, she leaped into the aisle and threw open her arms, ignoring the people nearby who turned to stare. Her intensity surprised him, and he was more than a little embarrassed as he waded through the watchful crowd to receive her embrace.

Six years had not changed her, not in any fundamental way. Her body was fuller, her face a little softer. In short, she had grown up. But she was still the same Jasmine he remembered. Her hair was piled up on top of her head, tied sloppily, as if she had done it with one hand on her way out the door. A few strands had gotten loose and fallen down around her shoulders with a sort of arbitrary perfection. That was the sort of beauty Jasmine possessed—effortless. Her hair and eyes were the same jet-black, very Spanish-looking. She wasn't Spanish, though. Something else. Turkish, maybe. Her skin was the color of milky coffee.

As they held each other, Charles could feel her breasts pressing up against him. The perfume on her neck smelled like lilacs. "It's good to see you again," she said. She stepped back and twirled around, as though wanting him to get a better look at her. Her dress was cut mid-thigh, made from a clingy, white material with ruffles at the bottom.

Someone at the bar whistled and Charles went flush, not knowing if he should say something. "Good to see you too," he answered, pretending not to have heard.

They sat down across from each other. Jasmine took a sip from her glass and set it beside another glass that was already empty.

A waiter passed and Charles ordered a beer. There was a lull where both of them looked around the room. Charles shifted in his seat and felt his leg rub against Jasmine's; he pulled it away instinctively.

"God, it's weird to be back," said Jasmine at last. She squinted and rubbed her chin as she looked around the room, as if conducting a scientific study.

"Is it?" said Charles. "I wouldn't know."

"Believe me, you'll see. Everything out there," she waved her hand at the rest of the world, "is totally different. Nothing changes here. It's terrifying. I had to stop by the mall this morning to pick up some things for Auntie, and out front by the bus stop were a bunch of skater kids sitting around on the curb smoking cigarettes and jumping their boards off the benches. Just like when we were in high school—same stupid, baggy pants and wallet chains and everything."

Charles shrugged. "How's your aunt doing?"

"Not good. She's got cancer."

"Jesus...what kind?"

"Stomach."

"That's supposed to be the most painful," he said, immediately thinking what an idiot he was.

"There's no cure for it," said Jasmine. "Not Auntie's, anyway. She's just way too old. All they can do is try to make her comfortable."

"Sorry, Jas."

Charles reached for his beer, but Jasmine misread him and took his hand, squeezing it from across the table. "I'll be all right," she said.

Charles asked if she wanted another drink and called the waiter over.

They talked late into the night, quite casually, as if it was the most normal thing in the world. Charles reflected that they had never been especially close during high school and mentioned this to her.

"What of it?" she said. "High school was terrible." She began rattling off a list of old names he had trouble remembering. Then she brought up Raymond, her high school sweetheart who had gone to California with her after graduation. Six months later he had moved back home, his tail between his legs.

"I would have loved to have been here for that," said Jasmine. "Four years of that 'big man on campus' shit, strutting around the school preening, and it only took six months away from home to cut him down to size."

"That's how it usually works," said Charles.

"How did I put up with him for so long?"

"You were young and dumb and beautiful. It was your duty."

She smirked. "And now I'm just dumb and beautiful."

"Not to mention modest."

Jasmine laughed. No girl that beautiful had ever laughed because of something he had said. The very sound had a profound effect upon him; he was like a man who had just popped out the door to buy a quart of milk, and on his way to the store had discovered his life's purpose. From the moment he had first received her phone call, a giant question mark had loomed in the background; he simply could not understand what had prompted her to contact him, to put toward him now such unprecedented affection. Such a rare and fragile thing this seemed to him that he dare not ask her directly, afraid their nascent bond would startle, take flight, like a deer from a hunter's clumsy footsteps.

They finished their drinks. Jasmine said she had to go. "I've got to be at the hospital at eight tomorrow morning."

"Good luck," said Charles. "I mean, I hope everything's okay with your aunt."

"I'll tell her you send your wishes."

"Does she even know who I am?"

"I'll explain it to her." She dug in her pocket. "How much do I owe you?"

"Don't worry about it. I'll play the gentleman."

"Thanks, love." She smiled and gave him a hug. "You have my number, right?"

"It's on my phone." They stood and made their way toward the exit, Charles—his hand on Jasmine's waist—guiding her through the maze of tables. When they reached the door, she made to leave.

"Wait a second," said Charles, "I'll walk you to your car."

"No, no, it's okay."

Charles hesitated. "Are you sure?"

"Yeah, I'm parked right out front. Good night!"

"Good night, then."

He watched the door swing closed. *Well, there it was*, he thought, as he went to pay the bill, *my first date in two years.*

Outside, Charles loitered in the faint glow of the café window, peering up and down the block until he was sure Jasmine had gone, before starting back toward his apartment. Night had crystallized, the air brittle and static around him; he clutched his lapels and pulled them together, burrowing deep inside his overcoat. It was times like these he regretted losing his car. Though only late October, a frost covered much of the sidewalk and made tiny prisms atop the handrails that lined the steps of the public school. What few leaves still clung to the branches of the beech trees lining the sidewalk seemed to lose their color and wilt all at once. A breeze began to kick up, a soft, lapping current that grew in intensity as he reached the first intersection, now whistling past his ears and searing his exposed skin. He dropped his head and trudged forward as the wind grew stronger, pushing back like some invisible hand against his chest.

How one's universe shrinks without a car! The café—twenty long blocks from home—had once been only a five-minute drive, a task undertaken with an almost autonomic lack of awareness. Now that he was on foot, however, it seemed to lay on some outer rim of existence, his own personal frontier past which everything would continue to remain a mystery, as distant and remote as if it were Timbuktu or Neptune.

Knowing how cold it would be that evening, he had considered asking Jasmine for a ride, but thought better of it. In America, a man was not a man without a car, and so he'd kept his mouth shut. Now he was making penance for his pride. Though he was the only one on the street at that time, Charles found little peace to be had; those more fortunate souls than he who still possessed automobiles roared past in endless procession, the growl of their engines mixing with the wind and the sputtering and coughing of the building generators to drown out any revelations he might have been blessed with at that late hour. A very noisy solitude.

Crossing street after street, then a gaping highway where four lanes of traffic sat snarling at him and the red light dangled over his head, Charles finally passed the oak-and-glass façade of the Japanese grocery on the corner of Vienna Street, where he lived. By now his stomach was growling—he had not had time to eat anything after work—and so he went inside, past the cash registers and the eternally frowning Mr. Yakamura, the owner, straight to the back of the store and the low shelves where they kept the cookies and pastries. Amid the rainbow panoply of glossy packaging, he finally managed to locate the yellow-and-white box that contained his favorite coffee cakes. Snatching them up, he studied the box greedily and started for the counter to purchase them, when his eyes happened on the red price sticker pasted on the side. Stopping, he dug into his pocket and counted up the money he had left over from the café: six dollars and fifty-two cents. That was his spending money for the rest of the week. Charles looked down at it, nestled so comfortably in the palm of his hand, then up at Mr. Yakamura in his striped angora sweater, arms crossed imperiously, staring back at Charles with barely concealed disgust. Paralyzed with indecision, Charles again looked down at the money, then at Mr. Yakamura with pleading eyes, but the latter stomped his foot and shouted, "You buy or put back!" As if woken from a trance, Charles skittered back to the shelves and replaced the cookies before hurrying out of the store, avoiding at all costs the piercing eyes that traced his retreat.

Outside once more, surrounded by the cold and with his stomach howling in protest, he stood rooted to his place on the corner; something inside would not allow him to go, as if walking away would validate the circumstances in which he now found his life. But his conviction was no match for the wind—it numbed his pride and tore at his cheeks until he was forced to admit defeat and hurry away.

Turning onto his block, he began to walk slower, more reflective now that he was so close to home and its relative warmth, and studied each building that he passed, the same ones he passed every day when he returned from work: on the corner, adjacent to the grocery, a massive, Queen Anne style mansion, all spindles and towers and eccentric flourishes; then, a series of stately Georgian townhouses in red brick, followed by a similar, second series of townhouses in the Federalist style; and after, reflecting a slight change of character, a long stretch of simple, stand-alone Colonial houses, each with a tiny green patch of lawn in front. Charles imagined what might be going on inside all these buildings, saw large feasts around dining-room tables, children being cajoled to finish their homework, couples curling up in front of fireplaces and other metaphors of domestic bliss.

Soon, approaching out of the gloom, he saw the chain-link fence that signaled the end of Vienna Street, allowing the driver no other choice than a right or left onto Industrial Park Drive, which, true to its name, skirted acres of hideous, midsize corporate offices that cluttered the horizon like ships in a Nicholas Pocock painting. Wedged in between the back of the CVS pharmacy on the corner and a row of sagging sugar maples was a squat, rectangular dwelling with dingy aluminum siding and a broken gutter. Around the back of this dwelling was a screen door, and through the door, down a set of concrete steps to the basement, was the room where Charles had lived for more than eight months.

It was an old-style basement in the fullest sense, which is to say it wasn't simply the subterranean floor of a house, but a place where the upstairs owner stored all the detritus twenty years of life had accumulated: old Christmas decorations and a plastic tree faded a sickly, pallid olive; several wooden chairs, each missing a leg or back slat; myriad cardboard boxes filled with bowling trophies, paint supplies, newspapers and other miscellanea; children's toys long untouched; miles of bright-orange extension cords; and shelves of rusty pliers, hammers and other tools. There was also the hot-water heater and the furnace that serviced the rest of the house and kept the basement warm enough that Charles managed to get by with just a small, electric space heater. The heater was one of the few things in the basement that belonged to him, along with a bed (which actually belonged to Barbara, the owner of the house, and was included in his rent); a single suitcase full of clothes; a nightstand (once more, on loan from Barbara); a reading lamp; a stack of old books and magazines; and a collection of travel posters and maps, which he had plastered over every available inch of wall space. All of this—his living area—was crammed into one quarter of the room. Catty-corner from his bed was a 'Pittsburgh Potty'—an exposed toilet and wall sink, along with a showerhead rigged up behind a wooden partition. Almost every old house in the city had one. In the old days, the mill workers would enter the house through the basement and wash off the soot before coming upstairs.

Everything was still in working order, and it was Charles's to use; for this, he paid three hundred dollars a month, but no electricity or water or utilities of any kind, and for ten dollars a week, Barbara took his laundry upstairs so she could wash and fold it for him.

There were times Charles was thankful to have found such an arrangement. To work in retail, he had learned, was to severely limit one's options. What nagged at him, though, was that in theory he should have been doing much better. He had full-time employment as a supervisor for a national electronics chain that was turning a healthy profit. For this, however, he earned only eight dollars an hour, which put him just on the edge of poverty. Though he managed to eat well, and to stay fit and well-groomed, and to get to work and back every day, the level of discipline it required was at times maddening. There was something exhausting, he thought, and damning to the soul about staring at a package of cookies in the supermarket, sick with hunger, trying to justify the expenditure of three dollars and ninety-nine cents. Something very much like despair. And then, to put those cookies back and to skulk home past the Queen Anne style mansion and the Georgian townhouses, feeling defeated even in this momentary victory over desire, as the windows, glowing with light and warmth, looked down at him like pairs of eyes passing judgment. How does one approach the world when even the end of one's own block seems like an unattainable dream? What keeps such a person going?

Charles shed his coat and sat down on the bed, though he felt too agitated to sleep. He turned on the heater and pulled it close, letting the warm air wash over him as his skin tingled to life. His eyes searched the room, though for nothing in particular; after eight months, he knew every corner and crevice of the basement by heart, as intimately familiar as if they were extensions of his own body. Lying back, he reached for the book he was currently reading, an early-nineteenth-century travelogue of sub-Saharan Africa. Suddenly he was in Abyssinia, trudging through the shifting sands of the Danakil, thorn bushes and the brutal sun pricking his skin as his team prepared to meet with Alli Manda, chief of the Dumhoeta tribe. From the center of his basement floor, there now sprouted an acacia tree, and the scent of hagenia and orchids tickled his nose. They marched northeast from Gondar, rising in elevation as the sun fell toward the horizon. There, on a windswept plateau jutting out from the southern face of Ras Dashen, three thousand meters above sea level, his team set up camp.

Charles slipped out of his clothes and crawled under the covers, staring up at the underside of the kitchen floorboards, his ceiling, as the minutes ticked by, imagining the African sky as he waited for sleep to come.

TechMart was more like a warehouse than a store, more than half a football field long and just as wide, with exposed steel rafters and finished concrete floors. Standing at the front of the store, near the registers (which was where Charles worked), one could barely discern the back wall rising hazy and indeterminate over the racks of discounted CDs.

With so much square footage under its domain, TechMart had developed a crude sort of feudalism to keep things running smoothly—each department was run as its own separate fiefdom, each giving fealty to the TechMart crown. In the back left corner was the music section, and next to it, on the right, was books. In the foreground, on the left, was computers/electronics, and on the right, movies. At the very front of the store were the cash registers, the section Charles supervised. All the other sections had supervisors too; they governed the day-to-day operations and filtered info to and from the assistant store manager, who in turn liaised with the store manager himself. At times, the supervisors had direct contact with the store manager, but generally only at his invitation. There were times, too, once every few months, when a mysterious someone called the 'regional manager' would appear at the store, an event—judging by the preparation and pomp that surrounded his visits—equivalent to a court visit by the Holy Roman Emperor. There were also constant references to 'corporate head-quarters', a shadowy cabal that, to store employees, existed only as a series of transcribed directives and whose existence was as faith-based as any deity. Such was the hierarchy that governed their lives.

It was a cold, drizzly Saturday morning, and business was slow. No more than a dozen people occupied the store, rudderless ships drifting from aisle to aisle with the watery, vacant stares of people trying to kill time.

The few hours before lunch were a time for silent contemplation; Charles spent them the way he usually did, leaning on the counter and staring out at the parking lot, where today a green Buick lazily stalked the spaces near the entrance. The events of the previous evening ran through his head on a continuous loop. Like an athlete studying game film, he dissected every movement, every word that had been spoken, trying to establish what exactly it all meant. He noted with some satisfaction, a swell of pride, that it had been she who had contacted him out of the blue. Whatever else one thought, that was significant. There had been nothing, however, in their conversation that suggested anything other than two people reacquainting. He combed his memory, trying to recall an instance where she had batted her eyes or perhaps played with her hair, some subtle hint. Yes, he was almost certain she had run her fingers through her hair, brushing it back, delicately, over her right ear. And the way she had asked him if he had her number—that was certainly an invitation to call her, wasn't it? Or else why would she bother to ask? But despite the airtight case he had built, he still could not get up the nerve to dial.

These deliberations were interrupted by a man and his girlfriend approaching the register. The man was tall and well-built, with a head like a moai statue and gelled bangs. The woman wore a Dolce & Gabbana sweat suit, bubble-gum pink. Her lips—bulging, glossy, burgundy-tinted—pouted at Charles from beneath her too-large sunglasses.

The man stepped forward and rapped his knuckles in a playful rhythm against the counter.

"Hey bro," he said, addressing Charles. "Can I do a return here? I wanna return something."

From a plastic bag he was holding, he removed and dropped a mangled CD case on the counter, the disc popping loose and wobbling to rest like a Frisbee in front of Charles. A large crack scarred the front cover and both hinges on the case had been snapped off. Charles picked up the item and made a show of examining it, then told the man he was free to grab another copy off the rack and he would make the exchange. Before he could finish speaking, the man dropped his gaze to the floor and held his hand palm out, like a traffic cop telling him to stop.

"No, no, no," he said. "Don't worry about it. I'll just take my money back."

Charles frowned. "I'm sorry, sir, we can't do cash refunds for open items."

The man looked up, eyes locked in an icy glare. "What do you mean?"

"I mean that since you opened it, I can't give you your money back. All I can do is give you another copy of this CD."

"Why would I want another copy of this CD?"

"Well, if it's broken, you can—"

"It's not broken...it sucks!"

Charles adopted his professional tone. "I'm sorry you're unhappy, sir, but unfortunately that doesn't change the situation."

"How's that now?"

"Sir, I told you, for open items, all we can do is replace the item if it's broken."

The man smirked and leaned forward, halfway across the counter, a slight menace in his expression. From this distance, Charles could see the signs of a painstaking grooming regimen: the meticulously plucked eyebrows, swooping out from the bridge of the nose in a perfectly comma-shaped arch; the pinkish, exfoliated, and moisturized skin, nary a pore in evidence; the teeth, bleached an eerie bluish-white and sanded to uniform length. Even his stubble had been carefully trimmed and edged. From the collar of his L.L.Bean jacket wafted the scent of Drakkar Noir.

"Why would I want to replace a CD I do not like?" the man growled, somehow making his question into a threat.

"You wouldn't," said Charles.

"Well then?"

Charles sighed and looked at the floor, the polished, checkerboard linoleum reflecting the arms of a ceiling fan overhead, a rhythmic strobe of light and shadow whose familiar vibration dazed him like a sunstroke. A tiny avalanche from the supply shelf beneath the register had left the area swaddled in plastic bags; they clung to Charles's feet like vines, no matter how often he kicked them loose.

"Look, I don't play in this band," he said, pointing to the CD. "I don't work for the record company that produced this album." The man looked at him with a dubious expression, and the woman—Charles noted with satisfaction—had stopped chewing her pinky nail and was listening attentively. "Therefore," he said, "it is not my fault you don't like the music. Does that make sense?" Neither of them answered, so he continued. "All the store guarantees is that the product you buy will be in working condition. So if the CD is broken, we will give you a new one. Otherwise, you might be taking advantage of us. You might be taking these CDs home and burning them, and then returning them for new ones."

"Burning them?" said the man.

"Right. I'm not implying that's what *you* do, but obviously *someone* could do that, and we need to make rules that take that into consideration."

"Did you say 'burn a CD'?" he repeated.

"Yes, but again—"

"Hey, honey," he said, turning to his girlfriend, "you ever heard of burning a CD?"

"What?" said the woman, scrunching up her face. "What!?!"

"Burning a CD. This guy said we might have burned the CD!"

"Burning a CD? What!?!"

"I know. I told him, why would I burn a CD? What does that even mean?"

"Like *burn* burn?" she said. "Is that what he means?"

"I don't know." The man leaned toward Charles again, subjecting his nose to another whiff of cologne. "Is that what you mean? Like *burn*? Does this CD look like it's burnt?"

The woman cackled and agreed that it didn't.

They continued back and forth in the same vein, voices steadily rising. A curious thing occurred then that reinforced Charles's belief that a guiding force did rule the universe and worked inexorably to make things more difficult for him. From this almost deserted store, a line had somehow formed behind the arguing couple. Whether everyone had simultaneously found what they were looking for, or whether they had heard the shouting and wanted a show, Charles now had a queue ten deep staring him in the face. Over the tops of their heads, he could see Ron, the assistant store manager, peeking out of the break room to see what was causing the commotion. Charles silently cursed, grabbed the intercom and called for backup, hoping he could get the line under control before Ron felt compelled to pay him a visit.

Too late. Even before he had put the microphone down, Charles could smell the stale coffee and nicotine and knew Ron was standing behind him. A pair of hands grabbed him by the shoulders and squeezed. "Everything okay?" said Ron, and immediately disavowed Charles's existence as he began playing kiss-ass with the couple, who presented themselves now as paragons of reason. The woman, Charles noted with disgust—this twenty-something trust-fund gym rat with her burgundy lipstick and panty line showing—started *flirting* with Ron, batting her eyes and giggling at his every word, and Charles knew at that moment he had already lost. Of *course*, the woman understood the return policy, and of *course* she would never dream of making a fuss over something so trivial, but they *had* come all the way from Youngstown, and when they tried to explain themselves this man (she pointed at Charles) had been extremely rude and hadn't bothered listening to *a thing* they said, and of *course* it was just an unfortunate misunderstanding, and so sorry for the disturbance they had caused. Not at all, assured Ron. It's always good to check on these things in person, and while store policy does state no returns for open items, each employee has the right to exercise discretion in individual matters.

Except me, thought Charles, though Ron had failed to mention that part. Charles felt as though he were an actor in a set-piece, hearing lines he knew to be a deliberate fiction and yet behaving as if he believed them. What made him stand there silently and accept such abuse, he wondered? The answer, of course, was his paycheck.

Ron told him to go ahead—just this once, *wink wink*—and give the guy his refund. Silently, Charles opened up the register and counted out thirteen dollars and eighty-seven cents, shrinking under the couple's triumphant stares. "Don't worry about it," the woman said with a smirk as he handed the money over, though he hadn't apologized. She mumbled something to the man and laughed as they strolled out the door.

"Let's get that line moving," said Ron. As he walked away, he added, "Stop by and see me when you go on your lunch break." For the next hour, Charles checked out customers in a sort of daydream, jaw clenching and unclenching, until one o'clock came and he went by Ron's office to see what he wanted. Ron was sitting behind his desk, staring at a computer screen and clicking repeatedly on the mouse concealed beneath his right hand. Any other time, Charles might have laughed; everyone knew that Ron had no real responsibilities—certainly nothing that required a desk and a computer—but his ego was still bruised by what had happened earlier. "Hey, there you are," said Ron, still fiddling with the mouse. "Have a seat." Charles sat down and waited, staring straight through Ron at a spot on the wall, using it to focus and keep calm.

"Cold out," said Ron, apropos of nothing, and didn't speak again for almost ten minutes as Charles sat watching the hands on the clock inch round. Suddenly, he sat bolt upright, locked eyes with Charles, and launched into a strange and wordy soliloquy about customer service, teamwork, and TechMart's corporate mission. From time to time his eyes shifted back to the computer monitor, and it soon dawned on Charles that he was reading a prepared speech. "You are the mortar in the pyramid of success," he said, pausing for effect. They exchanged glances, and Ron went back to reading. After several more platitudes, he concluded by informing Charles, almost as an after-thought, that this was his first official "corrective action", which would be noted on his performance review.

"But why do I deserve to be corrected when all I did was follow the company's return policy?" said Charles.

Ron pretended not to hear. He pressed a button on the keyboard and a sheet printed out, which he took and handed to Charles. He pointed to a line at the bottom where Charles was supposed to sign, acknowledging that the situation had been explained to him and that he had received his "first-offense remediation discussion".

"A fine ship you're running," said Charles, scribbling his name and tossing the paper back.

Ron shrugged and thanked him for taking the time to sit down and talk things over, stopping Charles on his way out the door to tell him to subtract the ten-minute meeting from his lunch break.

There were the two elderly men in hunting jackets, glimpsed through the potted ferns, eating a preposterously late breakfast. Over near a window that looked out on the back parking lot, a frazzled mother in a clunky wool sweater attempted to distract a pair of tow-headed youngsters with crayons and a placemat maze. Crossing the floor from the salad bar to the kitchen, an aging waitress with a still-passable figure stopped, grimaced, and reached down to adjust her shoe. What impressed Charles most, though, were not the people themselves, but the stark detail in which he viewed them; the lighting in the Crescent Diner was like a form of therapy, notoriously bright and revealing of all one's flaws. Not a single detail of any person or object was left unexposed from scrutiny. Charles wasn't exactly sure what effect the lights were having on his own psyche. He just wished the manager would turn them down a bit.

Like every other time he went there after work, Charles asked for a menu, studied it briefly, then ordered the same watery cup of coffee he always did. It was the cheapest thing on the menu, the refills were free, and as long as you kept drinking, they'd let you sit there all night. "Unless the place starts filling up," the waitress always warned him, a threat that—based on Charles's experience—was entirely cursory.

Across from Charles, Edmund—Charles's co-worker—was busy tearing open the packets of sugar from the plastic condiment tray on their table, pouring the sugar into a tiny mound, then using the edge of his driver's license to sculpt it, first stretching it out into one long ridge, then cutting the ridge into two smaller piles, then chopping them up into very fine lines as if he were separating cocaine. Edward performed this task in a sort of fugue state, as oblivious to what he was doing as a serial knuckle cracker or hand wringer. It was a habit Charles had been unable to dissuade him from, though it invariably left them short of sugar by the time their coffees arrived. Charles accepted it now as just another part of going to the diner after work. Once in a while he himself became hypnotized, watching in silence the tiny granules spilling and sliding over the Formica like waves upon the shore, bending and twisting from one pattern to the next, a fluid, ever-changing symbol impossible to pin down. Then the coffee would arrive, and the spell would be broken.

"Some fucking meeting today," said Edward, snapping awake as the waitress arrived with their cups.

Charles took his and thanked her, saw there was no more sugar left and consoled himself with two creams. "Same as always," he said.

"What did that mean, we 'must get a supervisor to sign off on all void slips before they can be rung up'? So if you're not working, I have to chase down Ron and get his signature on the slip? He's not even in the store half the time. Can I go to one of the other departments and get that supervisor to sign it?"

"Don't know," said Charles, taking a sip. "They never really explained how it's going to work."

"Fucking surprise." Edmund stirred his coffee, steam billowing upward as he made slow, languorous circles with his spoon, which clanked against the ceramic interior of the cup. "Just wait. We'll have lines all the way back to music. Then we'll get bitched at for not checking out the customers fast enough."

They continued in this way for twenty minutes, breaking down the new regulations and procedures that had been put forth at their weekly staff meeting and agreeing that none of them would work in practice.

This post-meeting roundtable at the Crescent was as much an institution now as the meetings themselves, and had probably done more to build morale among TechMart's workers than any of the corporate-sponsored get-togethers the store had implemented. Sometimes the attendance was small; sometimes so many people showed that they had to commandeer an entire section of the diner to seat everyone. Only Charles and Edmund had been free this evening, but regardless the number of people, the sentiment was little changed: management had no idea what it was doing, and they—the people on the floor, who actually ran things—were taken for granted.

Charles grinned as Edmund eviscerated the store manager's preposterously bad hairpiece, unveiled for the first time the previous Monday to a chorus of muffled laughter. Charles enjoyed these outings, which was fortunate, as they constituted almost the entirety of his social life. And yet, as satisfying as it was to be in the presence of other people—people who understood what he went through each day, and to whom could unburden himself—he couldn't help feel that something was missing. As Edmund continued, his acid tongue now targeting the manager's fashion sense, Charles found himself tuning out the conversation, lost in his own thoughts while he gazed out the window at the clear, autumn night devoid of motion.

For six years he had been complaining like this. People came, people left, and still he found himself exactly where he had started all those years before. Six years! Charles realized only a handful of people had worked at TechMart longer than he. For others this was a way station, a place to make some spending money while finishing school, or a second job to help pay off some bills. Something temporary. For Charles, though, it no longer felt temporary. For better or worse, this had become his life. That's what made these outings so bittersweet—complain as he might, the more he talked about work, the more attention he devoted to it, the more it consumed him. The line between work and leisure blurred more every day, and he noted with dismay that his date with Jasmine was the first time in years he had gone out with someone other than a co-worker.

He thought back to his good friends from high school and college. When was the last time he had spoken to any of them? They were spread out across the country now, seeds that had drifted far and put down roots in unfamiliar soil while he sat withering on the vine. The last time he heard from Gilbert Lamp, his best friend from all the way back in junior high, Gil was starting a job with a software company in California. He had described to Charles in breathless detail the perfect weather, the ocean, the superiority of West Coast girls, and the lifestyle to which his new pay and benefits were making him accustomed. "And what about you?" he had asked. "You still working at TechMart?"

"Same old story," assented Charles.

"Hey, don't sweat it," said Gil. "You'll be out of there in no time. Trust me."

That was two years earlier. It had never occurred to Charles until that moment that his job was something he should be worried about. He had a degree, after all, even if it was in something as unfashionable as history. He was still young and capable. The future was something that would sort itself out; it just needed time. And yet now, just weeks from his twenty-sixth birthday, he was the only one of his old roommates still living in Pennsylvania.

He looked across the table at Edmund, who was motioning to the waitress for a refill. Edmund was twenty, a junior in college. Six years was not a great divide, but Charles found he was already having trouble relating to the younger workers. They made constant references to bands and television shows, only a fraction of which he had heard of before, and their sense of humor struck him at times as juvenile and tiresome. Within a year, Edmund and most of the other students would move on, with newer, younger models coming in to take their places. Only Charles would continue to age. How would he relate to these people when he turned thirty years old, or, God forbid, forty? The only common thread connecting them would be TechMart. When that happened, his life would be subsumed.

Charles waved away the waitress's offer of more coffee; he had barely touched his first cup. Now he drank deeply, hoping the jolt of caffeine might jump-start his thoughts, help him make sense of things. Insanity, he had heard it said, was doing the same thing over and over and expecting different results. Charles thought back over all he had done the previous week, then the week before that, and marveled at the regularity of his days. One hardly need be prescient to know what the following weeks would hold in store for him. The key, then, was to change . . . something, anything. The only thing to happen outside his normal routine as of late was his meeting with Jasmine. Charles again thought about her number stored away on his phone. It had been nice seeing her, after all, nice talking with someone the same age who had gone to the same school with the same teachers, and who knew many of the same people.

"You okay?" said Edmund.

Charles blinked and looked across at him, realizing he'd been staring out the window again. "Yeah, fine."

"You've barely said anything all night."

"Just tired," said Charles, waving his hand.

He kept himself focused on the conversation after that, albeit with one foot out the door. His mind was made up. A sensation he had not felt in a long time, one of giddy anticipation, passed through him, like a swarm of grasshoppers vibrating in his stomach, then crawling down through his legs to the tips of his toes. The fear, the overwhelming joy of not knowing what might happen next filled him up like helium and threatened to lift him right out of his seat. He wanted to stand up and sing, but was too ashamed.

They talked well into the night. Though he could hardly wait to get home, Charles was far too polite to excuse himself early, and in truth the excitement he felt gave his conversation a sharp, incisive edge. The mundanities of work he dissected with a scholar's thoroughness; the controversy surrounding the clogged toilet in the men's bathroom that morning—and whose duty it was to fix it—he imbued with the subtlety and significance of a Byzantine political struggle.

When at last Edmund looked at his watch and suggested they ask for the check, it was already past eleven. Charles worried for a moment that he might have waited too long, that perhaps Jasmine was asleep already and wouldn't want to be bothered. He tossed his money on the table, told Edmund good night, and returned home determined. Scampering down the steps, he locked the door behind him, dug out his phone and found Jasmine's number, and sat down on the edge of the bed. At the precise moment he pressed the last digit, a wave of foreboding passed over him, a vague sense that he was making a mistake and would be better off forgetting the whole thing. He was on the verge of hanging up when he heard a *click*, and a woman's slurred "hello" came through the earpiece.

"Hello?" said Charles.

"Yes, hello?" mumbled the voice, again. "Who's calling?"

"It's me," he said, then, cleared his throat. "It's Charles."

"Charles?"

"Hello."

"Is that you?"

"Charles, that went to high school with you? We met at the bar last night..."

"For Christ's sake, I know who you are!" There was a laugh, cut short by a long, hollow yawn. "Your voice just sounds different, that's all. I'm sorry, I just dozed off before you called. I'm not all there yet."

"Ah," he said. "I woke you up." A pause. "So what are you up to?"

"I told you, I was asleep."

"I meant later on. What are you doing later on?"

"Tonight?"

In the background, Charles could hear the faint creaking of bedsprings. He pictured Jasmine stretched out across her mattress, rolling over onto her side to talk to him. "No, no, not tonight," he said. "I mean a different day."

"That depends on the day, I guess."

Charles stood up from the bed and began to pace. "Tomorrow? What about tomorrow?"

"Tomorrow I'm visiting my aunt."

"Are you sure? What I mean is, do you think you might be free? For lunch?"

"You want to have lunch with me?"

"If that's what you'd like..."

"Yes," she said. "I'd like that."

They made arrangements to meet near Charles's work the following day around one. She told him good night and hung up, leaving Charles to lie back on the bed and inhale the cold, damp air. A childish elation took hold of him; he had the desire to clap his hands, but held it in and continued breathing, deeply, letting the feeling mellow and subside into a serene, woolly joy, a thick blanket that surrounded him and filled him up, which the blaring TV and drunken muttering upstairs could do nothing to deflate.

From the nightstand, he grabbed an old *National Geographic* from the middle of the pile and thumbed through it, checking for anything he hadn't already read. A certain photo caught his eye; he had only glimpsed it for an instant as he flipped past, a burst of color in the midst of all that black-and-white print. Now he worked his way backward, one page at a time, trying to find it again. There it was, attached to an article profiling street vendors in different parts of the world—a tea seller in Marrakech, two rows of glasses stuffed to the brim with iridescent green mint leaves, and on top of each glass, a sugar block, arranged along a table draped in flowered linens. Behind the table stood the seller in white robe and fez, leaning over a stainless pot that belched clouds of steam into the afternoon air. He held a spoon filled with sugar, preparing to add the sugar into the pot.

Charles imagined speaking to the seller, hearing the unfamiliar words, made all the more unintelligible by the constant hum of conversation coming from the café behind them. He gestured to the pot and the seller nodded, then took down a glass and poured into it a pale, greenish liquid, into which he dropped a mint leaf. He offered it to Charles. Taking the glass, Charles put it to his lips and drank. A sticky sweetness enveloped his tongue, trickled down his throat and became a pleasant warmth in his stomach that soothed him and carried him off to sleep, where he dreamed of a woman in an elegant *djellaba* who held his hand as they walked in the shadow of the El Hank Lighthouse, along the edge of the sea.

———————

For months, Charles had been hounded by an evangelical Christian in a blue T-shirt. Whenever he arrived for his shift in the morning she was there, just as when he would leave on his lunch break, patrolling the sidewalk in front of his store with the diligence—if not the quiet stoicism—of one of Her Majesty's beefeaters. She had an indefatigably positive manner; Charles found himself oscillating between admiration and loathing for her, often within the span of a few seconds. Like a collapsed star, she allowed no one to escape her orbit. All were cornered and confronted and told the glorious news: "He is risen!" In place of a pike she clutched a wad of handbills, tiny manifestos slathered in biblical font, bearing provocative titles: "YOU CAN LIVE A VICTORIOUS CHRISTIAN LIFE!" and similar, hypercapitalized exclamations.

She was there when he arrived the next morning. Being that the store had yet to open, there was no chance of Charles slipping in unnoticed. The parking lots were still empty, and she stood there, in her blue shirt and khakis, scanning the distance, fidgeting like a puppy looking for someone to bound after. Charles circled around and approached the store from the side, keeping out of her line of sight for as long possible.

"Hello, good morning, sorry, sorry, no time, running late, gotta open the store!" he said, when his discovery became imminent. He hurried past her and dug in his pants pocket for the key, cursing himself for not taking it out ahead of time.

"That's OK, I can talk while we walk. Ha ha ha!" she said, chasing after him. "My name is Hannah—"

"I know that," said Charles, but she continued on, unfazed.

"I've traveled halfway across the country to deliver a message. A message that will *change your life!*"

They were in front of the door now. Charles dug deep into his pocket, his hand in well up past the wrist, searching frantically. Every time his fingertips encountered the key, it was invariably tangled in the pocket lining or obscured by the small stack of dollar bills he had taken out to pay for his lunch with Jasmine.

"The scriptures have spoken...you too can be saved!"

"Ah, here we go!" Charles produced the key and held it up triumphantly. "I'm sorry, I'm late for punching in."

He jammed the key into the lock, opened the door, and slipped inside.

"Take this to read!" cried Hannah, somehow managing to throw a pamphlet through the opening before Charles could shut and relock the door. She remained with her face pressed against the glass, hands cupped over her eyes, until she was sure Charles had picked up the pamphlet and was taking it with him.

As he passed through the breezeway and crossed in front of the registers to the break room, he saw her finally pull away and take up her post again along the edge of the sidewalk. He glanced down at the pamphlet: "YOU HAVE AN APPOINTMENT WITH DEATH!"

The morning passed quickly. Though there were only three hours from the start of his shift to his lunch break, Charles had expected them to crawl by as he waited for the chance to see Jasmine again. In fact, it felt like only a few minutes had passed when he looked up at the clock and saw that it was noon—only one more hour until lunch. He left his register and went over to where Hui Zhong, a college exchange student they had recently hired to work part-time, was sorting through the return bins.

His first thought for where to meet Jasmine had been the Crescent Diner, but its associations with work and with the everyday made him quickly dismiss it. It was then that he realized how limited his experiences were, because he could not think of a single restaurant other than the Crescent that was nearby; he had never had occasion to look for one. Jasmine had solved the problem when she suggested a steakhouse out on the highway, about a mile from the store. Still afraid to admit he lacked a car, he accepted and told her he would meet her there just after one o'clock, even though he knew there was no practical way he could make it there so quickly, let alone eat and make it back to the store in half an hour.

Charles looked down at Hui Zhong bent over the baskets of frayed books and unwanted movies, while she sorted them into sections, her long black hair tied back in a braid that stretched nearly the length of her spine. He waited for her to notice him, but she remained oblivious, engrossed by the task in front of her. Finally he cleared his throat and said hello.

"Oh!" she said, jumping to her feet. "You scared me!"

Charles blushed and stammered an apology. "I know we haven't had a chance to talk yet, and I wanted to introduce myself, especially since I'll apparently be your supervisor. My name is Charles."

He extended a hand.

"Hui Zhong," she said, with a smile and nod of the head. Charles noted the pronunciation: *Hoy-Zong*. He extended a hand and she accepted it, limply.

"I have a favor to ask you, Hui Zhong."

"You're the boss," she said, grinning.

"I take my lunch at one o'clock, but I'm going to be busy then and won't be able to get to the punch clock." He scanned the area to see if anyone was close by, listening. "I need you to go over there at one o'clock, take my time card and punch me out for lunch. Do you think you can do that?"

"Are you sure it's okay?" she said.

"Of course, no problem. I just need to pick up some supplies for the store, you see? So I won't be here to punch out at one. I'll be going straight to lunch after I get the supplies."

"I won't get in trouble?"

Charles winked. "I'm the boss, remember?"

"Okay," she said with a shrug, then went back to sorting.

At twenty minutes to one, there was a lull in the customers; Charles looked around and saw no sign of Ron. "Hui Zhong!" he said. "Open your register." Then, to the two people in his line, "She can help you right over there, on the other side." He put up his "closed" sign, tore the name tag from the front of his shirt, and grabbed his coat and gloves as he scurried out from behind the counter. "Don't forget," he said to Hui Zhong as he was leaving, "one o'clock".

"Okay," she said.

Outside, Hannah was busy trying to pin down people in the crowd who flowed around and past her, seamlessly, the way a stream circumvents a rock. Charles joined the current and ignored her as he hurried by. "Hey, did you get a chance to read the . . . " was all he was able to hear as he sprinted across the parking lot, making a beeline for the highway. When he reached it, a new dilemma faced him, as the highway possessed no sidewalks, forcing him to jog through the manicured patches of grass that fronted the shopping centers, and to hopscotch through the concrete maze of median strips and car lanes that made up the entrances to the parking areas. While engineered perfectly for cars, it was apparent to Charles that the designers of these monstrosities had never considered the possibility that a person might venture there on foot. It might even be argued that they had laid them out so as to be inhospitable to the man of little means and no automobile. Charles felt distinctly unwelcome, looking down at his damp, soiled shoes.

It was five minutes to one when he caught sight of the steakhouse. As he got closer to the parking lot he began to search for Jasmine's car, but couldn't find it. That lifted his spirits and he increased his pace; he had hoped to beat her there so she wouldn't see him approaching on foot. Beads of sweat dotted his brow. He hoped he had enough time to cool down and fix himself up before he faced her.

Charles reached the restaurant and stepped into a cool, pleasantly dim dining room. A square-toothed woman in a denim shirt met him there and proceeded to take him to his seat, a cushioned booth near the center of the room. He told the hostess he was expecting someone and could she direct the young lady to his table whenever she arrived?

"You got 'er," she said in a trumped-up cowpoke accent.

A dark cloud of a waitress drifted over to check if he wanted anything. He asked for a glass of water and told her he would order later. "I'm meeting someone," he said. The waitress turned and left without a word.

Charles looked around. Though he could count on one hand the number of times he had been in a steakhouse, he could tell right away that this was not a good one. The décor was vaguely southwestern, lots of brick and unfinished wood everywhere. Throughout the room, wooden posts stretched up to the ceiling, with long, iron nails pounded into them, from which hung such items as a horseshoe, a lasso, and even a metal washtub. The dividing wall that separated the two halves of the dining room looked like the front of an Old West saloon, complete with hitching post and swinging doors, which patrons and waitstaff alike were forced to shoulder their way through any time they needed to cross over to the other side. Even the floorboards were unfinished, wooden planks that went *clomp, clomp* whenever you walked on them. On each table sat a bowl of peanuts and a sign encouraging patrons to discard their shells onto the floor, a directive that had been happily followed judging by the leguminous carpet surrounding each of the chairs.

His glass of water arrived, a wedge of lemon impaled on its rim. Each time he raised it to his lips to drink, the ice cubes inside clinked together in a pleasing melody. He waited and he sipped and he checked his watch, then waited and sipped some more. At ten minutes after one the waitress returned, dour as ever.

"Are you sure you wouldn't like something to snack on while you wait?" she droned.

Charles sighed and looked down at his menu. "Just bring me a plate of six-shooter mozzarella bites," he said. "And another water, please."

"Would like some dippin' sauce with that?" she asked.

"Yeah, sure."

"Ranch or marinara?"

"Ranch."

"Okay."

The waitress skulked away, returning a few minutes later with a brightly painted ceramic dish, on which sat six very lonely-looking nuggets of fried grease. She was just setting it in front of him when the hostess poked her head around the corner and pointed in his direction. Then Jasmine appeared; noticing him, she half-waved and started toward his table.

Charles thought she looked as if she hadn't slept all night. Her hair was pulled up sloppily, long strands hanging loose at the sides, and her clothes had that baggy, slept-in look. Even so, she radiated a beauty that touched everything around her—even the restaurant looked less tacky with her standing in it.

"Hey," she said, touching his shoulder as she went around to the other side of the booth. "Been waiting long?"

"No, not too long," he said, glancing down at his watch. It was a quarter past one. His break ended in fifteen minutes.

"Traffic was hell coming over here." She tossed her bag into the corner and bounced across to the middle of the seat. "As I'm sure you already know."

Charles held out the plate and offered her a mozzarella bite. She grabbed one and tossed it whole into her mouth.

"What time do you need to be back?" she asked.

"One-thirty," he said.

"Oh God, so soon? I'm so sorry I kept you waiting here."

"It's no big deal."

"Do you want to just do this another time?"

"Forget it," he said. "I'm here now. If I get back late, I get back late."

Jasmine laughed. "Right on, screw 'em! It's only some crappy retail job anyway."

Charles took a drink of his water.

"There are about ten times a day I wish I could tell my bosses to fuck off," she said.

"Why don't you, then?" said Charles.

"Because you don't tell off the head of a major production company. Not if you value your career."

"Do you value your career?"

"It pays well," she said, shrugging. "I meet a lot of interesting people. Go to parties, fancy restaurants, different events...you know."

Charles snorted. "What would I know about any of that?"

Jasmine grinned sheepishly. "Sorry. I don't mean to sound the way I do. All I mean is that my job has its bad points, but I can't really complain considering everything."

Their waitress returned and they hurriedly chose some steaks off the menu.

"My treat," said Charles.

"No!" said Jasmine. "Don't be silly. I wanted to take you out."

"It's not gentlemanly to let the woman pay."

"Give me a break. You paid last time we were together, remember?"

"Are you sure?"

"I insist. I'm making you late for work, so I owe you anyway."

Charles threw up his hands in mock resignation and nodded. Inside though, he breathed a sigh of relief. The fifty dollars he had taken out of the bank for this meal was almost half his savings.

"So what about you?" she said. "When are you moving out to L.A.?"

He studied her, weighing her words. "Are you inviting me?"

"Well," she said, shrugging, "there are always places available. I'm sure you could find something cheap to get set up while you look for a job."

Charles fought to hide his disappointment, though what he had expected her to say even he wasn't sure. "I don't know. L.A.'s not really my type of city. I don't even know anyone out there."

"You know me!"

"I mean as far as finding work. I don't really have any contacts or anything."

"What's your degree in again?"

"History."

"So you're probably planning on teaching then? Is that what people with history degrees do?"

"Apparently they work at TechMart."

Jasmine snorted and began to laugh, a trumpeting alto that sliced through the gloomy dining area and cut to ribbons the conversations at the other tables. Charles felt his head go light, the blood in his stomach effervesce. It felt wonderful to be the cause of such a pure and joyful noise.

"But seriously," she said, "what are your plans? As far as your career and everything."

Charles wasn't sure how to answer. The truth was he had no plans, had stopped planning long ago. Exactly when he had quit thinking of the future (a future with options, with possibilities, that is) he couldn't say. There was no specific date or time he could point to as the moment he had resigned himself to life as a head cashier. It had just sort of happened.

"Honestly," he said, "I'm not even sure yet. Sometimes I feel like I have no idea what I'm supposed to be doing."

"Yeah..." said Jasmine. Her eyes dropped for a moment. "Yeah, I understand what you're saying. Sometimes I still talk about what I'm going to do 'when I grow up', you know? It's crazy that we're supposed to know exactly what we want to do with the rest of our lives. There are times when I think to myself, 'I should just ditch the movie business altogether and move to some random country to volunteer. Africa, Asia...anywhere.'"

A smile crossed Charles's face, and he slid his plate out of the way and leaned across the table. "Where would you go if you could move anywhere in the world right now?"

"Wow," said Jasmine. "I don't really know."

"Just pick a place. Where do you think you'd like to live?"

She twisted her mouth and looked up at the ceiling for a second before answering. "Japan was really beautiful. I don't know if I could stand eating seafood all the time, but Ginza—that was the neighborhood we stayed in—was really nice."

"You've been to Japan?"

"Uh huh. I went with some girlfriends of mine in college."

Charles felt a flutter, a mixture of elation and jealousy. "Where else have you gone?"

"Oh, I traveled around Europe for a bit..."

"Where in Europe?"

"France, Spain, England. I also spent a few weeks in Italy last year for this work thing, and got to see a little of Switzerland too."

"That must have been amazing."

She raised her eyebrows. "What, have you never gone abroad?"

"No, never."

"You should. I can't tell you how much I got out of it. How does that saying go—'The world is a book and those who don't travel read only one page'?"

"Right," said Charles, falling silent.

Just then the waitress arrived with their food. She set the plates down and asked if they needed anything else. Jasmine asked for some ketchup to go with her fries, and the waitress went to get it.

"Yours came with french fries?" asked Charles. "How come I got a baked potato?"

"Did you want fries?" asked Jasmine.

"Sort of."

"Go ahead and take one of mine."

"You sure?"

"Of course."

Charles leaned forward to stab one of the fries, but he couldn't get it on his fork. No matter how many times he tried it kept slipping away from him.

"Wait a second, let me help you," said Jasmine, picking up the plate and holding it out. Charles finally managed to hook a fry and brought it up to his mouth. As he did, he caught a glimpse of his watch—the time was one forty-five.

There was no sign of Ron when he returned to the store. Nor did he see Hui Zhong. Only Lee, a young man about Charles's age who usually worked in the music section, was at the registers. They exchanged nods, and Charles walked over to talk to him.

"Is he mad?" asked Charles.

"Who can tell?" said Lee. "Anyway, he's in his office. He wants to talk to you."

"Sorry you got stuck filling in for me."

"You can make it up to me later."

Charles left and headed toward the office, strangely unconcerned, knowing what awaited him. He felt neither fear nor elation, only "the lightness of the condemned man", as he had heard it called. Passing by the punch clock, he stopped and thumbed through the time cards until he came to his—Hui Zhong had failed to punch him out. Well, it hardly mattered now, he thought. He opened the door and went in.

Ron sat behind his desk, as usual, not looking at the computer this time, but sitting with his legs crossed, hands pressed together at the fingertips into a tiny steeple that

rested on his bulbous stomach. Two chairs sat facing the
desk at forty-five-degree angles. In the chair farthest from
the door sat Hui Zhong, her eyes downcast and cheeks
flushed a bright pink.

Ron gestured to the other chair. "Sit," he said.

Charles sat down and waited. Hui Zhong refused to
look at him, or Ron, preferring to fix her gaze at a point on
the floor, while her tiny frame from time to time quivered
with muted sobs. Her shame was evident; Charles recalled
a book he had read about the Chinese concept of "face",
and how in ancient times a young woman might be moved
to suicide by a simple slight on her character. Even this
passing thought was enough to transport him. Like
overlay transparencies, the colors and textures of the
book's photographs began to impose themselves on this
world, and suddenly he was no longer looking at a young,
modern girl in a red polo shirt, but a Han princess in a
bright vermillion *chaofu* robe. The drab functionality of
the office transformed into the plush, crimson-and-gold-
swathed splendor of a palace sitting room, Chin-era
paintings on silk hanging from the stone walls through
which a damp chill seeped and settled on Charles's skin.

Charles clamped his eyes shut in a physical effort to
drive off the visions. Soon the effect subsided, and he
found himself returned to the present day, where Ron and
Hui Zhong were both looking at him now with knitted
brows.

"Are you okay?" asked Ron, a hesitant concern in his
voice.

"I'm fine," said Charles.

"You looked like you were having a headache."

To his left, Hui Zhong had apparently forgotten her
shame and looked at him unabashedly, a mix of wonder

and loathing in her expression, as if he had been transformed into some rare monster. Charles wondered how long he had daydreamed this time, whether he had said or done anything he couldn't remember.

He had been daydreaming all his life, but never in public, never where others could see him, except for maybe his parents, who—entering the room unobserved—might have caught a glimpse of their son in the throes of what looked like a Baptist spirit-possession, muttering and making strange, jerky movements in response to a world not evident to the outsider. For all of his life, though, he had maintained a certain mastery over these fits; the presence of another, one whom he did not feel entirely comfortable around, had always been enough to break the spell, to suck him back through the ether into the world of the living. Now that had changed. Charles sat breathing, lips parted, paralyzed like a man who recognizes too late the lights of the train bearing down on him.

Their stares embarrassed him. Struggling through his confusion, he dug down and mustered the will to speak. "Just a small pain," he said. "They come and go. It's okay now."

"Well, if you're sure," said Ron. "I sort of hate that we have to do this now, when you're obviously not feeling that great, but . . . okay, look. I just had a talk with Hui Zhong."

At hearing her name, Hui Zhong once again flushed pink and averted her gaze, first looking down at the floor, then toward the wall, then back at the floor, as if even the various parts of the room were passing judgment on her. She squirmed as Ron detailed the conversation they had had, especially the part where she had come to him with a pang of conscience to ask if it was really all right for her to punch out Charles's time card. Like the closing paragraphs of a Sherlock Holmes story, Ron explained in clinical detail the shrewd line of questioning he had put to Hui Zhong, his collection of evidence—namely, the unpunched time card and Charles's absence—and of course his deductions.

All the while, Charles internally rolled his eyes and fidgeted, waiting for Ron to be quiet so he could admit his guilt. He had no desire to get Hui Zhong in trouble, and in truth, no longer cared what might happen to him. All he wanted to do was go home and sleep; the episode he had just experienced weighed on him. All else was a distraction.

Finally he was allowed a turn to speak. He admitted to everything—that it was he who had told Hui Zhong it was okay to punch his time card, and that he had left work early to meet a friend and had gotten back late. "All of it was my fault, not hers," he said, while Hui Zhong covered her face.

For coming clean and out of deference to his ill health, Ron took pity on Charles and stopped at issuing him his second official corrective action.

"But don't think you're just getting off the hook," said Ron. "Yearly performance reviews are coming up in another month. That's two black marks against you now."

Charles nodded and insisted he was aware of the gravity of the situation. Another acknowledgment sheet was placed in front of him, and again he scribbled his name on the line at the bottom of the page.

As they filed out to finish the rest of their shifts, the bright lights of the showroom made Charles and Hui Zhong squint and stagger forward like newly released prisoners readjusting to the sun. For the rest of the evening, Hui Zhong did not speak except to take care of the customers. She perpetuated her abject posture, as bowed and penitent as any monk's, right up until it was time for her to leave. Though she had avoided Charles at all costs throughout the day, still she was reluctant to go when the clock afforded her freedom; she gathered her coat and bag and walked to the exit, only to stop, her outstretched hand pressed against the door. Something held her inside. Her mouth moved, almost imperceptibly, as if rehearsing the message she wanted to deliver. At last she raised her eyes and turned to look, over her shoulder, only to find Charles looking back.

He hesitated, wondering if he should approach her, what he should say, but it was apparently too much for her; she threw the door open and ran off, a dream viewed through a picture window, receding across the rain-soaked parking lot.

After he punched out for the day, Charles crossed the highway to the supermarket. It always impressed him, stepping in through the robotic, swinging doors, how serene a place the supermarket was in the evening—the mentholated coolness of the air; the placid nature of the shoppers who grazed the aisles, scanning the shelves with Zen-like indifference; the elevator renditions of Herb Alpert wafting from the ceiling speakers at canary-whisper volume. They all combined to put him in a philosophical mood as he picked up some coffee, bread, cheese, and a few other staples. It was a feeling he wished he could take with him as he left the store with his bags and trudged over to wait under the Plexiglas shelter at the edge of the highway.

The days had grown noticeably shorter; dusk was approaching, and the concrete-gray sky made an unfortunate mirror of the city's drab, autumnal veneer.

Charles stood shoulder-to-shoulder with a pair of old ladies (also grocery shopping, judging by their bags) and stared down the road, searching impossibly among the sea of headlights for the two belonging to the F60 bus.

Soon (though never soon enough for the ones waiting), one of the pairs of lights came closer, and as it did, behind it, a large, shadowy rectangle appeared, which in turn soon clarified and crystallized into the shape of a bus. It came to a hissing stop right in front of them. Charles and the two old ladies clambered aboard and each chose a window seat from among the myriad available. The tint of the windows painted another layer of shadow over the city, turning Charles's thoughts gloomier as the bus pulled away again, heading now in the opposite direction from his apartment. They continued on for about a mile before turning off the highway onto a two-lane road that wound its way through a sea of well-tended lawns. The evening fog trailed like a scarf on the hedges and shrubs that skirted the properties. Every so often a copse of elm or maple trees slid past, with the ranch house it protected tucked safely in the background.

Another mile or so later the bus turned once again onto a gated street, this one with a giant signboard at the entrance reading "The Dales", and below it, in smaller letters "A Private Community". From a guard post on the side of the street, a man poked his head out and nodded to the bus driver before disappearing back inside. There was a metallic *clank*, and the white, steel gate in front of them began to retract, grumbling and groaning as it opened a path for the bus to continue.

The streets became narrower as they entered a tightly packed hamlet of two- and three-story houses, set on a plateau overlooking a pond, which glowed fiery orange with the rays of the setting sun. When they had circled around to the far side of the neighborhood, near the edge of the cliff where the plateau descended down into the valley, the bus made its last scheduled stop. Charles and the other passengers disembarked and headed off in different directions.

There were still a few people out at that hour, raking leaves and unclogging gutters, the endless domestic maintenance of fall. A few even sat on their porches, taking a final opportunity to welcome the night before winter chased them indoors for good. Charles waved and shouted a greeting to one such man as he turned onto Hemlock Street, the street where he had grown up. The man waved back and asked Charles how he'd been. Even now they still recognized him here, and though he lived only across town, his visits to his parents' house and the old neighborhood still had the feeling of a real homecoming, stirring within him a nostalgic longing for the old days.

The light was on in the living room at 62 Hemlock. Charles walked up the driveway—turning to squeeze through the space between his father's old pickup and the BMW his mother had recently purchased—and skipped up the steps onto the porch. After a couple cursory knocks he opened the door (it was never locked at this hour) and stepped into the breezeway. He poked his head into the living room and saw it was empty. From the top of the stairs at the other end of the hallway came the pitter-patter of footsteps descending. Charles walked over and turned into the hallway just as his mother, Helen, was coming out; she let out a scream and threw her hand over her heart.

"Jesus Christ, Charlie!" she said, panting heavily. "What did I tell you about waiting till we come to the door?"

He laughed and wrapped his arms around her while she calmed down. "Sorry, Ma. It's hard to get used to the idea I don't live here, you know what I mean?"

"You should at least call first," she said, squeezing him back now. "What's in the bags? Groceries? Come on, let's go to the kitchen. Are you hungry? Have you eaten yet?"

They went to the back of the house, to the kitchen. When they got there, they found Charles's father leaning on the counter across from the stove, pencil in hand, poring over a crossword in the local newspaper. He looked up when they entered.

"Mm, I was wondering who it was," he said, looking back down at his puzzle.

"Hi, Dad," said Charles.

"Hello, Son," said his father.

Even now, more than a year after his retirement, Charles's father dressed like he had just gotten out of a business meeting. Presently he wore a white button-down shirt with black slacks and a blue-and-gray striped tie. Over the back of the bar stool to his right was slung a discarded Brooks Brothers jacket, as if he had just popped in after a long day at the office and asked the missus what's for dinner. Charles had always seen this as a sign of weakness, that his father hid behind his clothes and his professional persona because he was too afraid to expose the real person underneath. Nevertheless, the image he projected was one of competence and confidence, and coupled with his broad shoulders, chiseled face, and closely cropped hair, the overall effect was something vaguely militaristic—intimidating to Charles, though he did his best to pretend otherwise.

Charles's mother shuttled him over to the other end of the room and sat him down at the kitchen table. "You want manicotti?" she said. "We've got plenty left." She scurried over to the cabinets and took down a plate, then over to the stove to scoop out a massive blob of noodles, cheese, and sauce from the casserole dish on top. "We've also got bread and salad, if you want some of those." She put the plate in front of him and made his father move over so she could grab a napkin and fork from the utensil drawer; these she brought back and arranged neatly alongside the plate.

Though he tried not to take advantage of his mother's goodwill, the smell of the manicotti was too much for his empty stomach to bear. He picked up the fork and began shoveling it into his mouth, greedily, bending low toward the table as if to lessen the distance between himself and the food. His mother stood slightly behind him and off to the side, smiling approvingly.

"If you get thirsty, there's water," she said. "And we have beer in the fridge."

"He's not touching that beer," growled Charles's father.

Charles heard the comment, but stayed silent and continued eating.

"For Christ's sake, Elton, he can have a beer if he wants one. You're not going to drink the whole case tonight."

"It's all right, Ma," said Charles. "Water is fine."

She looked at Charles, then over at his father, a thin-lipped frown creasing her face. Charles could see she wanted to press the matter, but thought better of it and went back to the cabinet to take down a glass.

As she filled it at the tap, Charles stole a glance at his father, still standing hunched over the counter, refusing even for a second to raise his eyes from his puzzle. Charles searched for some clue as to his temperament, to brace himself should the night take an ugly turn, but outwardly his father was placid as always. Rather than assuage his fears, it only made him more cautious, for Charles knew his father, knew the violent eruptions he was capable of, and where a stranger might look at a volcano and see only a benign mountaintop, those who grew up in its shadow knew the forces churning inside, ready to boil over and explode at a moment's notice.

Charles's mother brought him the glass of water, then took the bags he had brought for them and began putting everything away. "See what Charlie brought for us?" she said, rather loudly and insistently. This had been preceded by a pause and a sharp inhalation, as if she knew she was taking a chance making even this innocuous observation.

The question hung in the air for a moment, ignored by all, until finally Charles's father raised his eyes and cast a baleful glance over toward the cupboard, where Charles's mother was making space for a can of coffee.

"What's that now?" he said.

"I asked if you saw that Charlie brought us some groceries," she said. "Here's some coffee, some orange juice, some crackers..."

"Any cigarettes?"

"What?"

"Did he pick up any cigarettes?"

"What are you talking about?" she said in an annoyed tone. "You quit smoking. What do you need cigarettes for?"

"Just a question." He shrugged. "I wonder where he got the money for all this."

"From my job," said Charles, who had been listening silently, no longer eating but pushing the food around the plate with his fork.

"Of course," said his father, "your *job*." Charles heard the sneer in his voice, but did not respond. "That must have been expensive."

"It was," said Charles.

Behind him, over his left shoulder, he could hear his mother still arranging items in the cupboard, but more delicately now, as if the slightest sound might set off a conflagration that would envelop them all.

"How *is* work these days?" asked Charles's father.

"Fine," said Charles. "The same."

"No raises? No promotions?"

"Nope."

"Well, it sounds like quite a future you've laid out for yourself."

"I'm okay with it."

His father snorted. "Yes, you've made that abundantly clear."

"Elton!" barked Charles's mother.

In response, he shook his head and shrugged, muttering as he retreated back to the safety of his newspaper.

Charles's mother closed the cupboard and went over to the kitchen table. She pulled out a chair and moved it closer to Charles, sitting down and tenderly placing a hand on his shoulder.

"You do have other options, though," she said. Charles rolled his eyes and started to get up, but his mother held firm and eased him back into his seat. "Just listen, please," she said. "We're worried about you, is all. We can't figure out how you get by on so little. I mean, if you were to get sick or something were to happen to you, how would you deal with it?"

"I'd find a way," said Charles.

"No, you wouldn't." She reached out and took his hand, gripping it firmly. "We don't even know where you're *living*. God forbid there were some kind of emergency..."

"Ma, I told you, I have a temporary arrangement right now, but as soon as I move somewhere more permanent I will give you the address."

Behind him, his father chuckled. "He told you, Janine, he's just waiting for the designers to finish installing the granite countertops before he moves in, but as soon as it's finished he'll be sending out the housewarming invitations."

"Elton, would you please knock it off!"

"I find it revealing you equate granite countertops with respectability," said Charles, turning around.

"Oh, really?" said his father, his volume rising. "Please, enlighten me! Dissect my personality. You must have had a psych class or two in college, so try putting your fucking degree to use for once."

"It's not hard," said Charles. "You define success as the acquisition of material goods. Spirituality and personal growth mean nothing to you. You're really quite simple."

"I'm sorry, I didn't realize being a register jockey at some crappy electronics store was part of your spiritual journey."

"Sarcasm. That's all you've got."

"No, Son." Elton straightened up to his full height and looked Charles in the eye. It was all Charles could do to keep from visibly shrinking. "No, I'm completely sincere when I tell you I think you've thrown your life away. I don't find it funny, and I don't take any pleasure from it."

"I find that hard to believe," said Charles.

"I deal with things my own way."

"Yeah? So do I."

"Enough," said Charles's mother, "both of you." She sighed and put a hand on Charles's shoulder. "Now listen. I know you don't want to hear anymore about grad school, but I really think you should consider it."

Charles leaned his elbows on the table, cupping his face in his hands. "How is taking out another forty grand in loans going to help me, Ma?"

"It's for your education..."

"How am I going to get by when I'm barely making it now working full-time?"

"You know you've always got a place here. You could move back in temporarily while you finish school, and—"

"Over my dead body," said Charles's father.

"Goddamn it!" she cried.

Charles pointed at his father. "There's your answer, Ma." He stood up and pushed back his chair. "I've got to get going," he said, turning and striding out of the room without so much as a glance backward, the remainder of his dinner lying cold on the table. As he reached the breezeway his mother caught up with him.

"Charlie, wait!" she said. "We can work on him. Don't throw your life away just cause your dad's in a mood."

"It's not just a mood," said Charles.

"What do you mean?"

"I feel like we've been having this same conversation for years now."

"He just doesn't believe you'll follow through with it. But if you show him you're serious, that you're willing to do the work..."

"Who said I'm willing to do the work?"

She waved a hand. "You can handle it, Charlie."

"You're not hearing me," said Charles. "I know I *can* handle it. I can also get by just fine on my own, which is what I choose to do. So if you'll excuse me, I think I'll take a pass and head home now."

"Charlie..."

"End of discussion, Ma."

Charles knelt down to tie his shoes, right lace under left lace, then around and through the loop, all the time aware of his mother standing over him, wanting to reach out and gather him up in her embrace but aware that the time for such things had passed. She gazed down at him, and Charles watched her take in his sinewy arms and wide shoulders, his rigid jaw line and the bit of hair around his left ear where a few strands had gone gray, and let her arms fall to her sides. Whatever she had been about to say she discarded, and folding her hands in front of her waist, waited with downcast eyes for Charles to stand.

"Can I give you a ride?" she asked him.

"You don't need to do that," he said, though he dreaded the thought of taking the bus.

"Please."

Charles stood silent for a moment, then shrugged and nodded his head. "You want to see where I live?"

"I do."

"Fine. Let's go."

They went out into the chill night air and climbed inside the car, where the cold seemed to sink right through the layers of their winter clothes and settle on their bones. Charles's mother started the car. They sat there for a moment with the heater running, waiting for the shivers to work their way out of their bodies. Neither spoke. Neither turned on the radio. They sat side by side in the dim glow of the dashboard display, staring straight ahead at the garage door, illuminated by the car's headlights.

"Ready?" said his mother at last.

"Ready," said Charles.

She put the car into gear and glided backward onto the street. The neighborhood passed as a series of shadows as they drove, the only lights coming from the windows of the houses, small glimmers of life that had been bottled up, unshared with those on the outside. When they were halfway across town, his mother finally broke the silence.

"You know your father loves you, right?"

"I know," said Charles.

"He's worried about you. He just doesn't know how to show it."

They merged onto the highway, carving out a space in the bumper-to-bumper traffic that oozed southward, a creeping river of metal and plastic. Charles looked sleepily out his window, examining the faces of the people in the car next to him, until that car crawled out of view and he turned his attention to the next one. The faces varied in age and shape and color, but they invariably wore a similar expression of boredom and frustration. Charles shared the feeling; he wanted to lean out the window and introduce himself, to form some connection, something human out of this interminable night.

Next to him, his mother stirred in her seat. "Are you sure there's nothing I can do for you? Nothing you need?"

Charles thought for a moment. "I'm running out of stuff to read."

"Okay, then. The bookstore is right up here."

When they had gone a little farther they disengaged themselves from the highway and sped, like a dog loosed from its chain, up the entrance ramp to the mostly empty parking lot of the bookstore. It was rare that Charles had the time or money to visit one of these stores along the highway, and he felt a kind of thrill climbing out from the car and approaching the arched, glass doors, behind which could be glimpsed row after row of books stretching off into the distance, as seemingly endless as the ocean.

He felt a difference in his bearing as he entered, more erect, more dignified now in his role as consumer. Immediately he located the section where the travel books were kept—two long rows set between the U.S. history section and the public restrooms, near the café. The travel section was further divided into subsections; Charles was dismayed to find that three-fourths of the shelf space had been given over to guidebooks, those thick tomes of hotel and restaurant listings and tips for finding the cheapest cab fare. These could be safely ignored; designed as they were for the prospective traveler, they had no need to tell a story, as their audience would soon be experiencing a much more personal journey. Instead he stuck to the single bookcase devoted to travel essays, which—even as scant as it was in relation to the guidebooks—overwhelmed him with its choices.

There was no method he used in selecting his next book. Given his limited means, usually his books chose him. He depended on the charity of friends and co-workers, borrowing whatever they discarded, or the good nature of the head librarian at his local branch, a wigged and bespectacled old woman with a grandmotherly air, who every so often added a travelogue or two to the order sheet because she knew how happy it made him.

What faced him now was a rare and daunting opportunity. He scanned the neatly-stacked spines in front of him, reading through their titles, sipping them like a liqueur, savoring the fonts and colors till he was drunk on possibility. Over the public address system a crackly voice announced that the store would close in half an hour. Charles decided he needed a system to help him choose. He decided on a ground rule: he would not buy a book about a country he had already read about. That narrowed the field substantially. In fact, by the time he searched the final shelf, he had only found one slender paperback, a sort of journal written by a Peace Corps volunteer about his time in Bulgaria. Somewhere in his memory, Charles recalled seeing a photograph of a group of men digging through some sort of burial mound to look for treasure, which he believed had something to do with Bulgaria. Beyond that his mind was blank.

His mother stood behind him, waiting. "Is that the one you want?" she said. Charles nodded and handed her the book.

They went to the registers to pay; Charles noted with interest the computer system the cashier used, a modern touch-screen that put to shame the outdated Apple IIe he was forced to use. When the bookstore cashier pressed the total button and realized he had rung up the book twice by mistake, he simply reopened the transaction and deleted the erroneous amount. For Charles, this required filling out a void slip, hunting down a different supervisor to sign it, and starting the transaction over again from scratch. If he was so unfortunate as to make the same mistake twice, the entire process would have to be repeated. This had always annoyed him, but now that he saw the way things could be, he began to resent what was asked of him, that he should have to endure the scoffs, the insults, the complaints of so many customers just because his bosses wanted to save a little money. He took it as a personal judgment that even within the social hierarchy of retail, he and his co-workers occupied the bottom rung, not worthy of the smallest expense that might improve their lives.

His mother paid for the book and handed him the bag on their way out. "Thank you," he said, with genuine warmth. The rest of the drive home, Charles's mother beamed as she stared out the windshield, and it began to sink in for Charles just how much it meant for her to be able to help him.

Half an hour later they were in front of his building. Charles stood by the curb, leaning in through the still-open door to tell his mother good night.

"So this is it?" she said.

"This is it," said Charles.

She glanced absently at the house, then looked into his eyes. "My offer still stands. Any time you feel you need help, you're welcome to come back."

Charles thanked her again and kissed her on the cheek. Then he shut the door and started up the walk toward that squat rectangle with the broken gutter, toward ugliness, and behind it his room beneath the ground. The warmth of the car was already beginning to fade, and would soon be a memory in the cold darkness of the basement. *With a phone call*, he thought, *I could put an end to all this*. He pictured his old bed, warm and snug, covered in fresh linens. He imagined home-cooked meals, like the one he had just eaten, that filled his stomach in a way wholly foreign to him now. Most of all, he imagined another voice, someone to talk to when the monologue of his thoughts made him weary and despair going on even one more day. Yet he knew it was a call he would never make. Absurd as it was, something more compelling than his desperation prevented him from reaching out; he was like an animal, caged for years, that is suddenly presented with an open door, yet freezes on the threshold, more afraid of what freedom might entail than the captivity it knows.

As he circled around to the back of the house, Charles heard the whine of the car engine slowly fade off down the street. His mother was gone; now, the asceticism of daily life returned, swiftly and totally, as if his time at home had been the eye of some great storm, only a brief pause in which to catch his breath.

Charles went down the steps and into his room. Before he could get settled he noticed an envelope lying on the floor near the entrance, as if someone had slid it under the door. He picked it up and removed a piece of notebook paper. Scribbled on it in black ink was a message:

'Charles, please come upstairs and see me when you get home. Barb'

Charles sighed and checked his watch—it was almost ten o'clock. He thought about putting it off until tomorrow, telling her he had gotten in late and didn't want to wake her. That was a lie of course. He could hear the TV blaring right that instant, and he knew Barbara stayed up late Friday nights, Saturday being her day off from work. He also knew the day meant she had been drinking. Charles had rarely seen Barbara without a beer in her hand, but Friday nights were the worst. She drank with abandon, alone in her living room watching old movies till early in the morning, sometimes so drunk she yelled at the characters on-screen, a belligerent, one-sided conversation that claimed Charles—powerless to sleep against the noise—its only audience.

He decided to get it over with. The door at the top of the interior stairs he kept permanently locked and never used, lest he set a precedent where Barbara felt it okay to come downstairs whenever she wanted. Instead he went outside and up the steps to the back door of the house, rapping his knuckles noisily against the metal frame. After a short wait he spied a bit of movement through the glass, then the inner door swung open, and Barbara's face peered out at him through the screen.

"Hey there!" she said. "I was wonderin' if you would show up."

Sure enough, he could smell the alcohol on her breath, her words coated in a layer of stale hops and tobacco that assailed his nose. She leaned against the inside of the doorframe, dimly visible against the backlighting of the living room. It appeared she had just woken up—her hair, a greasy mop of gold ringlets, pressed flat against the side of her head. As was the case on the other evenings he had seen her, she wore an oversized sweatshirt, nonetheless inadequate to hide her enormous breasts or the roll of belly fat that hung down over the waistband of her black leggings, which were riddled with tiny holes and revealed every dimple and crevice of her ample legs and backside. She looked at him through puffy, half-lidded eyes, swigging every so often from the can of beer inside a foam cozy she clutched in her right hand.

"Come on in," she said, pushing the door open for him. They went through the darkened kitchen into the living room. To his left, along the wall opposite the TV, was a small couch made up like a bed, with sheets and blankets laid out over the cushions and even a pair of pillows propped up against one of the armrests; Barbara stripped everything off, revealing the green-and-white upholstery underneath, and pushed it into a heap on one side of the couch.

"Make yourself comfortable," she told Charles, sinking down on the newly cleared space.

Charles crossed the room and sat in the armchair near the front window. "What did you want to see me about?" he asked her.

She took a long swig from her beer and set the can down on the coffee table, empty except for a wrinkled, mail-order catalogue and an ashtray full of extinguished butts.

"Want somethin' to drink?" she said, and before Charles could answer she lumbered back to her feet and went into the kitchen, returning a moment later with a can of beer in each hand. She walked over and handed one to him. "About time for a refill myself." Charles was about to protest, but she waved him off. "Don't worry, drink up. There's plenty more where that came from. You workin' tomorrow?"

"No," said Charles.

"Well, there ya go," she said, raising her beer, "something to celebrate."

Charles raised his can as well, and they each took a drink.

After a short silence Barbara said, "You ever seen *Gone With the Wind*?" She pointed to the television, where Scarlett O'Hara was bent over picking cotton in the fields at Tara.

"A long time ago," said Charles. "What did you want to see me about?"

"My ex-husband looked a lot like Clark Gable," she said, as Rhett Butler appeared on-screen, languishing in an Atlanta jail. "Probably why I married him." She shrugged. "Probably why he cheated on me too." She paused, then said, "I need to talk to you about the rent."

"The rent? What about it?"

"I'm going to need it a little early this month."

"Early? How early?"

"As soon as possible." She took another long drink. "Tomorrow, if you can."

"Tomorrow! That's only the fifteenth."

"Like I said, I need it early."

Charles felt seized by panic. It had always worried him that he hadn't signed a lease when he moved in, but he had been desperate, and the low rent and convenience to work had been more than enough to convince him at the time. Still, he had feared a day like this might come. "I don't know what to tell you," he said. "I don't get paid for another week."

"I got someone comin' on Sunday to put in a new hot-water tank," she said. "I gotta have some way to pay for it."

"Can't you make payments?"

"Uh uh." She put the can to her mouth and tipped her head back, until Charles heard the last few drops being sucked from the bottom. There was a hollow *clink* as she set it back on the table. "My credit's a mess. I put half down up front, but I need to pay the rest when they get here on Sunday."

Charles covered his face and tried to think.

"Hey, look, I'm sorry Charlie," said Barbara, throwing up her hands. "I know it's tough, but we both use the hot water, and I haven't charged you a penny for it up till now. It's only fair."

"No, no, I understand. It's just I only have maybe a hundred bucks in my savings account. That's it. Could I give you a little bit now and then pay you back?"

"Maybe we can work something out," she said. "You need another drink?"

"I've still got half of this one."

"Finish it up. I'm going back to the fridge."

She left again and came back with two more cans of beer. This time, instead of walking one over to him, she put his can on the coffee table next to hers. "Come over here and sit. There's nowhere to set your drink over there."

Charles hesitated, but at last he got up and went over to the couch, not wanting to offend her.

The space on the opposite end from Barbara was taken up by the pile of blankets; she reached over and patted the middle cushion.

"Right here," she said. "Sit down."

Charles turned to squeeze through the narrow space between the couch and the table, shuffling across to the middle where he sank down next to Barbara. He was immediately pulled towards her, her weight causing such a depression in the cushions that no matter how he shifted, he could not keep from pressing up against her flank. Barbara simply leaned back, making no effort to move away, and turned her attention back to the television.

"I don't know how many times I've seen this movie," she said. "It's nice, like having back the good parts of my husband without the other ninety-nine percent." She laughed, warm and beery, against the side of Charles's face. "He really did look like Clark Gable, you know. I was quite a looker too, twenty years ago. Loads of guys were after me in those days, but what can you do? Time goes by." She put her drink down and turned toward him. "Don't worry about the money. We'll work something out."

All of a sudden, Charles felt a hand on the inside of his thigh, creeping higher and higher, up between his legs, and then Barbara leaning in towards him, her lips caressing his neck, then sucking, her tongue dragging over his tender skin and leaving long, slimy trails wherever she mauled him, like the footprints of a snail. Charles wrestled an arm loose and jumped up from the couch, knocking back the coffee table and spilling beer onto the floor.

"Come back here!" screamed Barbara as Charles ran out the door. "You owe me money!"

When he was back in his room, he locked the door behind him and sat on the bed. Perched right near the edge, he kept his feet raised up on the balls ready to spring, as if sitting had been some disagreeable obligation undertaken for form's sake, like visiting a distant aunt over the holidays. Any moment, he expected to hear knocking at his door. The absolute silence in the room struck him, a gauzy, suffocating silence that had the inverse effect of amplifying every bump and knock and miniscule vibration, and he realized then that he had been holding his breath. Adrenaline flooded his brain, giving his thoughts both randomness and clarity. It was all over now. He would have to move. His mind worked feverishly to come up with an escape plan, brainstorming places he could sleep that night, to the metronome of his heart thundering against his rib cage. Above him he could hear the thump of footsteps and the vibrating screech of the coffee table being dragged across the floor. He traced the footsteps as they crossed the living room, into the kitchen, then returned to the living room again, several times, until at last Charles began to realize that she was not coming after him. Still, sleep was out of the question; his entire body stood at attention like a rabbit's ears at the approach of a fox, and as he grew more and more bored with waiting, he began thinking about the new book his mother had bought for him, desiring to dig it out of the bag and devour the first chapter, but too afraid that Barbara might interrupt him in the middle, as if his reading were a state of undress or some equally compromising position.

To satiate himself, he took to scrutinizing the maps spread across the wall over his bed, searching the European one directly above his pillow until he had pinpointed Bulgaria. It was a tiny, green nub sandwiched between yellow Romania to the north and purple Greece to the south, its eastern border nevertheless managing to nuzzle up against the Black Sea's murky waters like a piglet carving out space at the trough among two massive hogs. It was a political map, telling one very little beyond the aspect of nations' borders; still, Charles saw that Bulgaria's northern border was demarked by the Danube River. These words were like a cognitive trigger, releasing a torrent of half-digested, half-remembered information he had imbibed over the years—the Danube is the second-longest river in Europe, it passes through four capital cities, it once formed part of the Limes Germanicus, which kept the barbarians out of Rome . . . and then there was the Black Sea, about which he knew very little, with its sinister name that conjured up images of ghostly pirate ships and death.

Drowsiness began to set in. Tentatively, he removed his shoes, then stripped down and got into bed. The footsteps had stopped, replaced by the television turned to full volume, accompanied by a strange muttering that grew louder throughout the night. Charles relaxed and let his head sink down onto his pillow, imagining what tomorrow would bring, while upstairs Barbara roared at Vivien Leigh for stealing her man.

Early the next morning he phoned Jasmine to tell her he had the whole day free.

"I have to go by the hospital soon," she said. "Do you want to come along?"

"Of course," he said, though he hated hospitals and felt strange visiting a woman he had never met before.

"Great. You just want to meet me over there?"

"I've got to run to the store first," he lied. "They forgot their keys and need me to open up for them. Maybe you could stop by and we could ride over together. If it's not too out of your way, I mean."

"No problem," said Jasmine. Charles hung up, splashed some water on his face and hurriedly dressed. On his way out, he closed the door softly and tiptoed up the stairs. He knew there was little to worry about, though. Barbara would sleep well into the afternoon.

Walking out toward the highway as fast as he could, sometimes breaking into a jog, which he would cut short the moment he became conscious of it, he reached TechMart a few minutes later and stood at the far end of the parking lot to wait for Jasmine.

After some time—Charles had lost track how much, staring out at the cars whizzing past—a silver Lexus pulled into the lot and circled around to pull up beside him. He waved to Jasmine through the tinted windows before opening the door to get in. She was dressed more simply this morning, jeans and a purple sweater. *This is how she would look if we were dating*, he found himself thinking.

They pulled out onto the highway.

"I told Auntie you'd be coming. She seems to know who you are. Or at least who your parents are."

"I wonder how," said Charles.

"Who knows? Everyone seems to know everyone in this town."

The hospital was not far away, just off the highway between the Century Mall and a bank processing facility. If not for the large sign reading "Saint Vincent Medical Center" there would be little to distinguish it from any of the adjacent retail complexes; it had a generically boxy design, conceived by and for administrators rather than patients, who would find little to be inspired by in its drab, minimalist veneer. Jasmine parked in back and they walked around to the twin sliding-glass doors of the emergency unit.

Inside, Charles found it to be like any other hospital, with the same off-white walls and the smell of finely scrubbed and disinfected misery. Through the entrance, off to his left, was a waiting room. A man with a bandage tied to a large gash in his forehead sat in one of the moth-eaten chairs, holding a clipboard and filling out a stack of forms. Three or four slightly less dire patients sat near him, all filling out forms as well.

Just past the waiting room, on the right, was the reception desk. A nurse with a bulldog face approached them and asked what they were here for. Jasmine told the nurse her name and who she was there to see, and signed them both into the guestbook.

The cancer ward was on the East Wing, eighth floor. They walked down a long, bustling hallway where nurses and physicians scurried from room to room, seemingly at random, as if no one knew which door led to which patient. At the end of the hall on their right was an elevator inside a glass shaft. They got in and pressed the button marked "eight", looking down on the parking lot as they were carried up, the cars and the people steadily shrinking with each floor they ascended.

They stepped out into another hallway, less frantic than the first but even more crowded. About half the people were staff and half patients. Charles could tell them apart by their clothes; their faces all had the same sunken, weary expression. They weaved through the crowd, took a left at the next hallway and stopped in front of room 804.

"This is it," said Jasmine.

Abutting the door was a small window. Charles stopped and peered through it before going inside. He saw a closet-sized room with a single bed, in which lay an old woman he did not recognize. She had steel-gray hair, as fine as silk thread, pulled into a tight bun at the back of her head. Her skin resembled an old cutting board, scarred with deep wrinkles. There was a vitality in her eyes that age and sickness had done nothing to extinguish. Even though she lay there half-lidded, she looked less like a tired old woman than a great mind in the throes of contemplation, the way a grand master looks hovering over a chessboard as he studies his position.

Jasmine opened the door, and he followed her in. The old woman gave no indication she noticed them. They moved a bit closer, right up to the side of the bed. Jasmine touched her aunt lightly on the shoulder. "Auntie," she half-whispered.

"What?" said the woman, and blinked her eyes as if waking from a dream.

"It's me, Auntie. How are you feeling?"

"Oh...hello sweetie." Her aunt's voice sounded exhausted, but she managed a smile. "I feel fine. I must have dozed off."

"Auntie, this is my friend, Charles," said Jasmine. Charles stepped forward and extended his hand. "You remember I told you about him. Charles, this is my aunt, Eleanor."

"Nice to meet you," said Charles.

"You're Janine's boy," said Eleanor, pressing her tiny hand into his palm.

"That's right. How did you know my mother?"

"Oh, when she was little she used to run around with the Hendrickson girl who lived next door to us. I saw her all the time. I used to go to school with your grandmother, too."

"Grandma Ruth?"

"Yes, Ruth." Eleanor shook her head, eyes clenched. "A shame what happened to her. So young. How is she doing, your mother?"

"Good. Still living in the same house, over in The Dales."

"That's good." She looked back and forth between Jasmine and Charles. "And how do you two know each other? Are you living out in Hollywood too, um...I'm sorry."

"Charles, Auntie," said Jasmine. "I told you before, we went to high school together."

"And you're still living here, Charles?"

"That's right."

"I thought maybe you two were dating."

Jasmine rolled her eyes. Charles, despite himself, felt his cheeks turn red. "Auntie..." said Jasmine.

"What?"

"No one 'dates' anymore, Auntie."

"No? What do they do?"

"We're not a couple, if that's what you mean," said Jasmine.

Eleanor shrugged and let the subject drop while Jasmine helped fluff her pillows and brought her a glass of water from the restroom. When she was comfortable, Jasmine and Charles sat and kept her company, making small talk about the staff—which nurses were kind to her, which weren't—as well as the banality of the food and the view of the clouds out her window, the totality of her ten-by-twelve-foot universe. She asked the two of them about their lives and other matters taking place outside the hospital as if they were events in another country, so far removed from her understanding as if to be abstract. There was a childlike wonder to how she greeted developments already years old, such as Jasmine's cell phone, which she turned over and over with the gingerly touch one might reserve for a rare Faberge egg, while her great-niece talked about things like "3G networks' and 'Bluetooth capability", a futuristic language as arcane to her as Sumerian.

When they had stayed two hours, Jasmine told her aunt she was hungry and that she and Charles were going to get lunch. She promised to come back in the afternoon to visit some more, a take-out bag in tow.

"Oh, thank you, sweetheart," Eleanor said, laughing. "I'm sure going to miss you when you head home."

"I know," said Jasmine. She leaned over to kiss her aunt on the cheek. "But I'll still fly back whenever I have a break to check on you. And these home attendants are really the best. The people we talked to just raved about them."

"I know, dear. I'm sure it will be fine. You're too young to spend all your time in hospital rooms waiting on an old lady anyway."

"*Auntie . . .*"

"No, it's true. This is the best time in your life. I want you to be happy."

Jasmine gripped her aunt's hand. "I am happy. I'll see you after lunch, okay?"

Charles said his good-byes and followed Jasmine back out to the car. "So, that's Auntie," said Jasmine, as they got in and closed the doors.

"She's nice," said Charles.

Jasmine started up the car and glided back out onto the road. "I'm just going to grab some sandwiches from the deli, if that's okay."

"Yeah, fine." Charles stared out the window, his mind fixated on something that had been said in the room. "What did she mean when she told you she was going to miss you?"

"Oh, I haven't told you yet, have I? I'm heading back to California next week."

Charles felt his throat catch. "You're leaving?"

"Yep. Auntie's being discharged in a couple days. We hired a home attendant to take care of her. She really wants to be back at the house, and honestly, her treatment's not having much of an effect. None of us are really sure how much longer she has."

Charles felt a profound longing, the suddenness and severity of which he had not expected. Like a brush fire, it spread to every corner of his body, starting at the stomach and fanning out through his shoulders and knees to the furthest extremities, a terrible rending, as if his very cells were tearing apart from each other. He tried to speak but could not find his voice. Even his breathing felt labored, a pneumonic heaviness gripping his chest, pressing down on the ribs like the talons of some giant creature.

"Charles? What's the matter?"

Rendered mute, he turned back towards the window and focused on the metal lampposts skipping past at regular intervals, allowed the sensation to pass through him until it gradually loosened. "Nothing," he managed to say.

"This is what Auntie wants," she said, misreading his thoughts. "I didn't come up with this myself. If she wanted me to keep taking care of her, believe me, I would find a way to make it work."

"And so that's it? You're going home next week?"

"Yeah, that's right."

"And what am I supposed to do?"

His words trailed off at the end, having left his mouth before shame or pride could check them.

Jasmine's eyes narrowed; she shot furtive glances in Charles's direction in between watching the road. "What are you talking about?" she asked him.

"Just what I said." Charles began to speak more clearly, his voice gaining the confidence of his convictions. "What am I supposed to do when you leave?"

"I don't know. The same thing you're doing now."

"No..." He shook his head. "I can't live like this anymore."

"Okay, so do something else then!" she said, sounding exasperated.

"Like what?"

"Why are you asking *me*?"

"Because I can't stop thinking about you."

She rolled her eyes. "Oh God, *Charles*..."

"I mean it. Ever since you got in touch with me, I've thought about you non-stop."

"We hardly even know each other."

"I want you to stay. Here, with me."

"How would that even work?"

"I don't know!" His voice rose, plaintively, his hands waving about like a conductor leading his orchestra. "Just stay, that's all!"

"And do what? Work at TechMart?"

"No..."

"Or are you going to support me on your salary while I stay home?"

There was a sarcastic edge to her voice. It cut Charles like a knife, and he turned in his seat to more fully face her. "Look, Jas, all I meant was that I really like you, and—"

"It's not going to happen," she said.

Charles pressed his lips together, silent, contemplating what she had said. After a few minutes he nodded, slowly. "I know."

"Then why would you ask me that?"

"Because I had to," he said with a shrug. "Because I've got nothing else, nothing to lose."

"For Christ's sake, I only called you because I've been gone for six years and hardly know anyone and I wanted to go out and have a good time while I'm here. I'm not looking for a relationship. I'm certainly not going to throw away everything I've worked for to move back to Pennsylvania to be with a guy I had a few drinks with one night at some crappy café."

"It ... doesn't have to be here," he said. "I would go with you if you asked."

"I'm not your savior, Charles. If you're unhappy with your life ... "

The thought ended, abruptly, a problem without its solution. Jasmine raised her hand from the steering wheel in a dismissive gesture and drove the rest of the way in silence, only speaking again as they approached their exit to ask Charles where he wanted to be dropped off. His stomach rumbled a reply, but he didn't dare remind her they had been on their way to get lunch. Even now, as he sat there exposed and naked, his pathetic entreaties dismissed, he found that pride would not allow him to let her see his true circumstances. The shame of poverty was too great, and he told her to return to the store, concocting a story about retrieving the keys he had taken there that morning to unlock the doors. Jasmine pulled into the lot and let him out.

"Take care of yourself," was all she said before pulling away, leaving him no time to even say goodbye. Exhaust fumes enveloped him, filling his nostrils with a flinty odor and clouding his vision while the car shimmered away into nothingness; Charles threw an arm over his face, wiping his eyes clean with his shirtsleeve. When he looked up again the car was gone, evaporated like a desert mirage.

He stood there for a moment, regaining his bearings, staring around him at the world as if reacquainting himself. He thought about where to go next, what to do, but remained inactive, a body at rest running solely on inertia. An old proverb popped into his head, one he had learned in high school and used to repeat over and over in an attempt to appear mysterious: "If one's words are no better than silence, one should keep silent." It occurred to Charles that this applied to movements too—if one's movements were no better than stillness, one should keep still. Unable to think of a single person or matter that required his attention, he decided to remain where he was, frozen in space until compelled to move again.

Like the reels of an old projector, his imagination began to spin. He saw himself standing there on the pavement, staring off into the distance with Zen-like detachment while devotees placed flowers at his feet, and a gaggle of onlookers and media types asked each other what it all meant. His vision, however, was destroyed by the blaring of a car horn, and a sky-blue Buick that pulled out around him, from which a man's head appeared and cursed him for blocking the exit lane.

That was enough to start him moving. His first few steps took him back in the direction of his room. Like clockwork, he remembered the book his mother had bought for him, still waiting on his nightstand. A warm front had rolled through that morning, giving the air the lush, almost balmy feel of Indian summer. Though he could not exactly enjoy the weather, he appreciated the break it provided from the constrictive cold that had plagued him for weeks. He walked taller now, freer, no longer thinking of Jasmine except to register surprise at how little he thought about her. It was a thought, admittedly, he had distressingly often.

Only when he came back to the book, pictured its slate-gray, matte cover with the illustration of an old man driving a donkey cart and its title, *Going Na Gosti: My Bulgarian Journey*, slathered across the top in Breughel font, was he truly able to exorcise her image altogether. He thought about the author, C. Evans Fulbright—a preposterously blue-blooded name for a Peace Corps volunteer—and about the Peace Corps itself, an organization that seemed to belong to another era, and which, like the Foreign Service or Merchant Marines, he had always viewed through a romantic lens, imagining a society of detached and worldly young men wandering the globe having grand adventures laced with the danger and lustiness of exotic climes.

When he arrived home and opened his door, he found for the second straight day an envelope lying on the floor. His stomach knotted as he bent down to pick it up. Inside was another note from Barbara, written in a terse, legalistic manner:

> *Mr. Lime, this notice is to inform you that your payment of $200 for purchase and installation of a new hot-water tank at 158 Vienna Street is due no later than October 18. Failure to provide payment on time could result in adverse action against you, including possible eviction from the aforementioned address.*
>
> *Sincerely,*
> *Barbara Hagel*

The letter shocked him, not as much for what it portended as for the fact that Barbara possessed the ability to write it. Had she contacted a lawyer, he wondered? If so, why? They had no lease. She could throw him out whenever she wanted. Only then did the dread begin to set in. October 18 was Monday—only two days away. Two hundred dollars would wipe out his bank account. Then rent would be due in two more weeks, and that would be that. No amount of number-crunching could save him— the shortfall was spectacular and unavoidable.

Charles had heard it said that it was easier to deal with a situation devoid of hope than one in which hope exists, that rather than proving crushing it allowed the sufferer to let go, to surrender to forces beyond his control and achieve a blissful harmony with the universe. Like most philosophical maxims, he found the truth in it cold comfort when the situation applied to himself. Panic seized him as he shut the door and sat down on the edge of the bed, looking around in wonder that such decrepit surroundings could produce in him so much longing.

His eyes eventually fell on the nightstand, and the book that had dominated his thoughts just a few moments ago. Snatching it up, he immediately felt calmer, like a soothing balm had been spread across his nerves. The spine he held in his left hand, using his right thumb to fan the pages like a cartoon flipbook. Then he turned the book over to read the synopsis on the back, and a pair of blurbs from two writers he had never heard of before—"Fulbright could make a trip through my kitchen sound epic. A writer of rare wit and sensitivity," said Jaromir Woodcock, author of *Czech, Mate! The Trials and Tribulations of a Czech-English Upbringing*. In the top-right corner was a photo of C. Evans Fulbright staring moodily up at Charles, his face a mixture of aggression and wonder, as if he were gazing upon a unicorn he wanted to pummel. Underneath was a short author bio—Charles was shocked and dismayed to find that he and Fulbright were nearly the same age. Now that he had something against which to compare, his life's shortcomings stood out in stark relief. That there were those in their twenties who had already published books and traveled the world was not news to him, but he had only ever considered it before in the abstract. Those prodigious, young writers he did know of were from an earlier era, all old men by now, if not dead, more like myths than real people and hardly someone against whom he could judge himself. Now here was a contemporary, looking not all that different from Charles, who had accomplished all that Charles hoped to accomplish in his lifetime. With some trepidation, he opened the cover and turned to the first page, afraid what other existential blows might await him inside.

"Landing at the airport in Sofia..." it began.

————————

Landing at the airport in Sofia, we clambered off the plane into a bare and cheerless terminal, a first impression that seemed to confirm all of the stereotypes I had had about post-Communist countries—the boxy architecture; the overwhelming grayness, as if it were perpetually overcast, even indoors; the dour customs official, who stamped my passport with a frown and regarded my cheerful "thanks" with stony suspicion.

We had just arrived after a nine-hour flight, seven hours from D.C. to Frankfurt and two hours to Sofia. For many of us, myself included, this was the first time we had ever been outside the United States, other than the odd trip up to Canada. Not only were we leaving the United States, but we were not coming back for more than two years—twenty-seven long months in a country none of us knew anything about. Fifty of us—full of the exhilaration that comes with flinging oneself headlong into the abyss, having severed ties with family and friends and all the other lines of our safety nets—marched confidently, exuberantly through this coffinlike terminal, as conspicuous and brash and American a parade as ever there was. Even now, I wonder what the locals who stood there staring at us thought of it all. I remember being aware of their eyes following us wherever we went, but it brought me no embarrassment; like a true American, I took it for granted that I would be the center of attention, and reveled in my quasi-celebrity status.

That feeling was only heightened when we gathered our luggage and stepped out of the atrium into a barrage of flashbulbs and television cameras. Every media outlet in the country, it seemed, had sent someone to cover our arrival. One of our program directors, a tall, bony middle-aged man with a crew cut named Phil, took control of our group and led us in a charge around the media's right flank, toward a tour bus that sat patiently waiting for us by the curb. As we filed past, microphones were shoved in our faces, accompanied by questions in Bulgarian or broken English that were equally hard to make out. All of the reporters seemed to be female, lithe women with dark hair and high cheekbones who followed us along the sidewalk on impossibly high-heeled shoes with the grace and balance of cats. More than anything, I wanted to talk to them, but our orientation coordinator strictly forbade any interaction with the media until after training, when we had gained some familiarity with the language.

On the bus, spirits ran high. We chattered away with the easy camaraderie of a football team after a victory. Greta, a recent college grad from Indiana, skinny and tomboyish, her brown hair in pigtails and tiny brown freckles on her cheeks, marveled at the cameras. "I've never even been in our local paper!" she said. Alfred, a retired math teacher from Oregon, short and round, bald on the top of his head but with small tufts of gray hair around the ears, sat looking out the window in a sort of lovesick stupor. "I can't believe I'm in Bulgaria," he said, grinning. "This is amazing!"

The bus pulled away, and we were off, first down a four-lane highway reminiscent of our interstates, if not for the strange makes of cars—Lada, Skoda, Moskvitch—*that coughed and sputtered around us like a cloud of asthmatic flies. Soon we veered off into the city itself, passing through a neighborhood of dingy gas stations, industrial plants, and fenced-off car lots, until I began to think I had been transported to some forgotten quarter of Newark. There were differences though, immediately felt but not immediately apparent. There was less fear in the air, none of the seething undercurrent of violence I had felt in American cities, yet it also lacked a certain vibrance, a sense of being alive and of possibility, as if everything, from the people to the trees to the buildings, were simply waiting around to die. Later I would understand this as a product of poverty and the way it was shared, a thing completely unlike America's vast wealth gap. I would also come to find that working beneath the surface were small pockets of young people carving out a niche for themselves, places where the creativity and energy needed to transform the country had room to breathe. But at that time all I knew was the slow burn of misery outside my window.*

Then, with almost no transition, the cityscape vanished, and we were surrounded by evergreens and rolling hills that made me feel like I had been transported back to my native Pennsylvania. I saw, too, for the first time, a typical Bulgarian house, as you would find in any small village or scattered across the countryside. It was a squat, one-story, brick structure, the walls covered in a type of plaster so that none of the brick was exposed, with a reddish-

orange roof made of Spanish tile. This particular house was surrounded by a spacious yard several acres big, the grass patchy and untamed, on which grazed a small flock of sheep, munching lazily. At the side of the house was a vegetable garden being tended by a crooked, wrinkled old woman in a peasant dress and headscarf, looking as if she had stepped straight out of a century-old photograph. Later, when we passed through the village of Pancharevo, I saw similar houses bunched closely together, side by side, along narrow dirt-and-gravel streets. An iron fence set into a low concrete base completely encircled each property, with a swinging iron gate at the front to let people in and out. Even the comparatively small yards inside these fences contained gardens. Many had animals as well: chickens, goats, and even, inexplicably, a full-grown cow camped out beneath a carport, staring at us benignly as our bus rattled past.

We started to climb, following a narrow two-lane road as it snaked its way high up through the Rila Mountains south of Sofia. Fir trees surrounded us on all sides. The August heat we had found so oppressive on disembarking the plane steadily dissipated; soon we were shivering, our bus passing through thick banks of fog that seemed to seep in through the windows and settle, cold and damp, on our skin. As we continued climbing, the road became a thin ribbon gripping the mountainside. To our right a sheer wall of rock passed by mere inches from our faces; to our left, just past the edge of the opposing lane, with no guardrail for protection, the ground abruptly fell away, plummeting thousands of feet to the gold-green valley below. We gazed out our windows in silence, brought on in equal measures by our reverence for this untouched gem of nature and our fear that death lay just around the next corner.

Perhaps I should pause for a moment to describe for you the phenomenon known as the Bulgarian driver. Ostensibly, Bulgaria possesses traffic laws just like the United States, but I have yet to see anything on the roadways that would verify this fact. Speed limits are routinely ignored, not just on the highways but on the tiniest of village lanes. Passing is treated more as an obligation, to be achieved at any cost, than an option reserved only for when circumstances merit it; at one point on our mountain journey, our bus—approaching a bend in the road past which nothing could be seen—suddenly veered into the left-hand lane and proceeded to attempt to overtake a Volvo, which had the temerity to be driving only twenty miles per hour over the speed limit. As our bus was traveling twenty-two miles per hour over the limit, this was totally unacceptable. For nearly three agonizing minutes we navigated this twisting road in the wrong lane, barreling toward blind corners, careening toward the edge of the cliff, while all the while the Volvo kept almost even pace with us, exhibiting a similar nonchalance towards the possibility of being crushed like a soda can against the adjacent rock wall. I am not sure if it was divine providence that in those three minutes not a single vehicle happened to be traveling the other direction on our stretch of road, but the driver considered it validation enough of his ability and judgment, which had been falling under increasingly hysterical criticism from my fellow travelers and me.

As is no doubt evident from the fact that you're reading these words, we survived the journey and, after turning down a long dirt road that took us deep into a forest, arrived at the Hotel Scorpio in the resort town of Borovets, which was to be our lodging place for the following week of orientation and training. A slight drizzle was falling as we staggered out into the cool mountain air, lush with the scent of ozone and pine . . .'

Charles blinked and looked around. Something was not right. He took a deep breath, but the pine scent was gone. The rain and the bus and the trees were gone too. It was then that he realized he was no longer in his room reading, but outside, wandering the sidewalks of a neighborhood he did not even recognize. It was late at night; the moon loomed high overhead, casting a silvery glow over a row of shops to Charles's left, all gated and locked for the night. To his right stood a stone railing. Peering down over the edge he could see the waters of the Connoquenessing Creek oozing past, glittering like some dark jewel in the moonlight.

Other than Charles, the area was deserted, the only sound the hum of the streetlamps up above. At the end of the street was a convenience store with its lights still on. He went in and asked the woman behind the counter for help, astonished to learn that he was in Riverview, a neighborhood across town from where he lived. Try as he might, he could not remember how he had gotten there, nor did he remember putting on his coat and his shoes, which he now realized he was wearing. The book he had been reading was gone; he wasn't sure if he had brought it with him and misplaced it or if he had left it in his room. His feet and legs ached, which made him believe he must have walked the entire way. A million questions plagued him, but he realized his first priority was to get home. He asked the woman if any buses were running, and when she said no, asked her to call him a cab.

The ride back took twenty minutes. Charles had just enough money to cover the fare. When the cab was gone, he approached the house with some trepidation, his skin tingling the way it had as a child when performing one of his friend's elaborate dares. A sense of foreboding hung in the air, as if he were revisiting the scene of some gruesome crime. He had no reason to expect he'd find anything other than his room, exactly as he had left it. Yet he felt afraid all the same.

Going around back, he tiptoed down the stairs and slipped his key noiselessly into the lock. Cracking the door an inch, he put his eye to the opening and peered inside. The room, of course, was exactly as it always looked. Breathing easier, he pushed open the door and went inside. On the floor at the side of the bed lay the book he had been reading. Other than that, nothing was out of place. He picked up the book, put it on the nightstand and collapsed on top of the covers, feeling suddenly exhausted. The more he tried to sift through what had happened to him that evening, the more his body rebelled, his eyelids drooping in dogged protest. Taking out his phone, he saw it was nearly three in the morning. He reached over and put the phone next to the book on the nightstand, after which he immediately fell asleep, dreaming of a bus ride through a misty mountain forest he had never visited before.

———

The following morning he awoke to the trilling of sparrows. It was a sound he had not heard in weeks, ever since the vicious cold that had moved down from Canada had locked the town in frozen suspension. It gave him a pleasant sensation as he stretched and rubbed the sleep from his eyes, as if winter had decided to abdicate this year and usher in an early spring.

Charles lay staring at the ceiling, feeling well rested from the previous night, the events of which he had still not begun to comprehend. He understood, obviously, that something was wrong, but what it was—and what to do about it—left him baffled. A medical disorder seemed a likely culprit, though physically he felt superb. Still, he resolved to call a doctor and set up an appointment just as soon as he returned from work.

Charles shot up out of bed and grabbed his phone, his heart sinking as he flipped it open and looked at the time— ten-thirty. He had forgotten to set his alarm. Not bothering to wash or change his clothes, he made sure he had all his things and ran out the door at a sprinter's pace, not slowing down until he had reached the highway, where the heavy traffic prevented him from crossing for several minutes. He waited on the corner, hopping from foot to foot like a boxer in training, until the light finally changed and he took off running again, across the road and the parking lot to the entrance of TechMart, where a handful of people milled about at a distance, out of range of Hannah's pamphlets, as they tried to figure out why the store had not yet opened.

The crowd swelled forward when Charles unlocked the door, peppering him with questions. Among the crowd were the other employees who were scheduled to open, including Edmund, who came up to him and asked what had happened.

"I tried calling you and everything, man," he said.

Charles checked his phone and saw he had two missed calls. He paused for a moment to catch his breath. "The volume was off," he said. "I never remember to turn it on."

"You better hope Ron doesn't hear about this," said Edmund.

Charles felt his heart skip. "You didn't call him, did you?"

"No. I think Bea wanted to, but I talked her out of it."

"Thank you, Ed. Seriously, I owe you."

"Just watch it from now on. Our performance reviews are almost here. Oh shit," he said, backing away, "here comes that Christian girl."

Out of the corner of his eye, Charles saw Hannah walking over to stand beside him. "Hiya," she said.

"Hey," said Charles, keeping his eyes averted.

"Oversleep today?"

"Yep."

"I didn't see you yesterday."

"It was my day off," said Charles, fighting with the lock.

She ducked her head down and tried to catch his eye. "I missed you."

"Thanks."

"Did you get a chance to read the pamphlet I gave you?"

"Yep."

"How did you like it?"

"I liked it."

"Yeah?" Charles could almost hear her grinning. "What was your favorite part?"

"The end."

She laughed. "Mine too!"

There was a *click*, and the door swung open. The crowd heaved a sigh of relief and barreled forward, almost knocking Charles down in the rush to get inside. He started to follow everyone in when he felt a piece of paper being placed in his hand. "Just something else you might be into," said Hannah. "Enjoy your day!"

He glanced down at the cover as he went in: "COMPLAINING WILL ONLY MAKE THINGS WORSE!"

When he had the registers up and running, he left Edmund to cover the front and went around the store to deliver the returns from the previous night. Specifically, he wanted to go to the book section to talk to Bea, to apologize for being late and to convince her not to mention anything to Ron.

Bea was a high-waisted woman in her late forties with regular features and a thick mane of brown hair, like a horse's. She even owned horses, on a farm she shared with her brother in upstate New York. Charles found her hastily applying lipstick at her kiosk, and said hello. He started making small talk, asking a lot of questions into which he dropped terms like "quarter horse," "furlong," "closing stretch," and "Missouri fox trotter," whatever he could recall from the handful of horse races he had seen in his life. Bea informed him that she raised horses for riding, not racing, but she began to loosen up. Charles used the opportunity to ask about her father, who had just gone in for bypass surgery. He recounted what his grandfather had gone through with his own quadruple bypass, happy for the opportunity to speak so frankly and knowledgably on such a serious matter, and to offer some hopeful words beyond the banal assurances that "everything will be all right." By the time he got around to apologizing for being late, thrown in almost as an afterthought, Bea just shrugged it off.

"Don't sweat it," she said. "Everyone has an off day. I just hope Ron's not so cheap he won't give us the forty minutes back on our time cards."

Charles froze. He had forgotten about the time cards. They would all read "ten-forty." And it would be up to him to offer an explanation. Dejected, he walked back to the registers and bided his time until Ron showed up for the day. There was nothing to be done. No time to concoct a plan to save himself. He simply sat watching the clock, counting down the minutes until a quarter to twelve.

When the hour arrived, Ron appearing like the Angel of Death, Charles did not hesitate. Before Ron could reach the door to his office, Charles accosted him by the punch clock.

"I was forty minutes late opening the store," said Charles.

Ron blinked and turned around. "Huh? What's that?"

"I opened up late. I wasn't feeling well, and I overslept. Look at the time cards," he said, pointing.

Ron squinted at him, seeming unsure what to make of such forthrightness, before turning to examine the cards. "Hmm," he said. "These are all forty minutes late."

"I know," said Charles.

"What happened?" said Ron, turning to look at him.

"I told you, I slept in," said Charles. "I wasn't feeling well last night. I must have slept right through my alarm."

"Mmm hmm," said Ron, making his disbelief evident. "Didn't anyone call you?"

"They tried. I must have slept through it."

"Because you weren't feeling well," said Ron.

Charles started to answer, hesitated, then merely nodded.

"You look okay," said Ron.

"I feel much better now."

Ron clicked his tongue and looked down at the floor, pondering something, leaving Charles to sweat and fidget in the intervening silence. Finally he looked up and said, "Any reason no one called me when they couldn't get a hold of you?"

Charles shrugged. "Maybe they didn't want to bother you."

"Okay," said Ron, opening the door of his office. "We'll talk about this later. When is your lunch break?"

"One o'clock."

"See you at one-oh-two."

Charles went back to checking out customers, thinking to himself that it was time for a change. No more being hung up on Jasmine or any other girl, he resolved. No more wasting entire days lost in some old magazine. From now on he would be the model employee. He would show up early and stay late. He would volunteer for the dirty jobs, cleaning clogged toilets and customers' vomit. He would fill in for others who needed the day off, take extra shifts without ever asking for overtime. He would swallow abuse from management and the public, speak always with a smile, and do whatever was necessary to ensure the satisfaction of all those he served. He would work his way up through the ranks, little by little, scrimping and saving every penny he earned, until one day he had built the life he always dreamed of.

By the time his lunch break came, he could hardly wait to see Ron to tell him of his recommitment to the company. He went to the office, knocked on the door, and went inside. Ron was sitting at his desk, typing something out on the computer.

"Is this a good time?" asked Charles.

"You're fired," said Ron, without looking up.

Charles said nothing at first, either not hearing or not understanding what had been said. "I'm sorry?"

"I'll need your keys and your name tag." Ron patted the desk with his hand. "Don't bother finishing out your shift. It's already covered."

Charles couldn't remember the last time he was free on a Sunday afternoon. He struggled to remember what he used to do with his free time. Poor people, he reflected, have worse memories than the rich, deprived of the landmarks by which to judge time's passage. All of life lived in the same place, following the same gray routine, made time immaterial, and nostalgia a fatal extravagance that distracted from the here and now. When something threw a wrench into that routine, the result was paralysis.

Charles wandered out of the store like a case of shellshock. Even Hannah kept a respectful distance as he passed.

After going home and trying to read for a bit, he found he could not concentrate. Some invisible hand compelled him to take the bus all the way down to the lakeshore, where he strolled in near-solitude beside the white sand and the boats docked in the marina. Staring down at the dark green waves lapping against the wood, he felt melancholy. He was not angry at losing his job. Nor was he distraught. Rather, he felt a long, slow ache in his stomach, a hopeless sense of watching the inevitable occur, like a chess player who sees he's beaten after ten moves but is forced to play out the tragedy to the very end. He had a dreadful feeling that where he was now was exactly where he was supposed to be. Where others might have found comfort in the absolution such an idea offered, it chilled Charles to consider that he might never make a better life for himself, no matter how hard he worked at it.

Sitting down on a public bench, its rubber-coated-metal seat digging into his backside, he watched a flock of geese out on the water glide gracefully around each other in overlapping circles, like Shriners in their tiny cars. Chaotic as it looked at first glance, their movements took on a certain pattern, an intricate interweaving of figure-eights that nevertheless seemed to serve no higher purpose. The geese would bob their heads every so often to nibble up bits of flotsam from the water.

Charles wished he had a loaf of bread with him to crumble and throw on the grass. He imagined it now, the geese gliding over towards him on shore and stumbling out of the water on those spindly legs of theirs, so gawky and self-conscious out of their element. The idea was so pleasing to him that he began checking his pockets in hopes that he really did have some food he could offer them. All he found, though, was the book he had been reading. It was stuffed into one of his back pockets, done, presumably, on his way out the door. He couldn't remember bringing it with him, nor could he figure out how he hadn't noticed it before when he sat down. The cover was creased, the pages bent into a "U" from all the weight pressing on them. Charles bent them back the other way, rolling the book up like a newspaper as he tried to flatten it out. When he had it more or less back to normal, he opened it and skimmed through the pages, until a passage near the middle of chapter eight caught his eye and he began to read:

Zemen was the name of the town where I was stationed, a word that translates roughly into "earth" or "soil". It was an appropriate choice for a moniker, as what little industry Zemen supported consisted chiefly of mining operations, digging into the hillsides that surrounded the town like some granite soup bowl, harvesting gravel. The more I think about it, if I were to sum up this community of two thousand souls in as few words as possible, I could hardly do better than "it was a town named 'Dirt' that exported rubble". Anything one might wish to surmise about the character of Zemen—its people, its climate, its architecture, etc.—would be found in the spirit of that quote.

My living quarters were the top floor of a two-story house, owned by a woman named Maritsa, who was my counterpart at the obshtina—or "city hall"—where I would be working as a "community development advisor" with the local government. She was in her late-fifties, a grandmother lacking the least grandmotherly sweetness, with her slightly hunched shoulders, wrinkly skin, and face like a moray eel. Though the house possessed no interior staircase—to go upstairs, one had to go outside and climb the steps at the side of the building to a separate porch and entrance—it was still a common occurrence to find her tottering around my kitchen at all hours of the day in her nylon hunting vest and baggy sweatpants, a Victory Gold cigarette dangling from her lips. "Charlie," she would say (that is how my Bulgarian friends referred to me), "sedni! Haide hapni si malko chorbichka!", and on the table would be a steaming bowl of orange broth, in which floated tiny bits of chicken meat, gristle and bone, as well as carrots, potatoes, peppers, and a massive hunk of soft, white bread sitting alongside it waiting to be dunked. In truth, it was excellent soup, and on the rare times its appearance coincided with my hunger, I was grateful beyond words. The other 90 percent of the time I felt under siege, my privacy a relic of another place and time.

Maritsa's house sat atop a dirt road on one of the hills surrounding the town. From my porch it was possible to look out over all of Zemen's rooftops, a sea of Spanish tile, all the way across to a hill on the opposite side of town where the monastery of Saint John the Theologian stood tall and stoic, returning my gaze as if we were two, solitary spectators in the upper levels of a coliseum. Just past Maritsa's house, where the road terminated in a severe, granite cliff rising straight up into the sky, were the operations of Metalurg Mining Co. Morning after morning, pickup trucks full of big, sullen men would rumble past our house and deposit their cargo inside Metalurg's gates. The men, looking dazed, would stretch and yawn and stand around in groups, *toeing the ground, smoking cigarettes and occasionally mumbling a sentence or two in another's direction, as if they believed themselves to be in a café despite the lack of chairs and tables and waiters bringing coffee. Eventually, at some unseen signal, the groups would begin dispersing, each man gathering up his equipment—picks, hammers, shovels—and clambering resignedly up the rocky hillside.*

One Thursday afternoon we had the day off from work. (To an American, a surprisingly common occurrence; besides the plethora of holidays and "name days"—days on which a particular Orthodox saint, and everyone else bearing that name, are celebrated—it was not out of the ordinary for government offices to close simply because the mayor desired a big lunch, or because the secretary had to pay her Internet bill in the neighboring town of Pernik, two hours round-trip by train, and really, what can get done without the secretary being there anyway?)

I had already showered and was sitting at the kitchen table, delighting in the breeze filtering in through the open window, while Maritsa stood over the stove boiling coffee in a metal urn. Bulgaria inherited its coffee from the Turks—a black, viscous substance like tar that went down one's gullet with the smoothness of battery acid. When ours was ready, Maritsa filled two porcelain cups about the size of shot glasses and brought them over to the table. Into mine, I added a teaspoon of sugar, then stirred up the concoction and drank it down in one quick gulp, gagging at the end on the grains that had settled to the bottom of the cup and now stuck to my tongue and teeth, as if I had swallowed a mouthful of sand at the beach.

Through the open window came the familiar growl of truck engines. Maritsa explained that the miners weren't as lucky as us and had to work that day. (I believe it was Dimitrovden—*the name day for "Dimitar".) She suggested we take a walk over to the worksite so I could introduce myself to everyone; being a* 'community development advisor', it would no doubt benefit me to make the acquaintance of those in the industry responsible for the community's existence. Having nothing better to do that day and inspired to action by the coffee—what it lacked in taste and texture, it more than made up for in potency—I agreed.

We put on our shoes and trudged up the dusty path. The sun was already flexing its muscles at this early hour, burning off the last of the morning mist seemingly before our eyes. We arrived at the gates and I felt somewhat uncomfortable as we shuffled inside, approaching the workers who stood at the foot of a towering conveyor, as always in a tight cluster, mumbling inanities as they awaited the signal to start their day.

As we got closer the mumbling stopped, and all eyes turned to stare at us. Almost two months into my service, this was an aspect of life in Bulgaria I had yet to acclimate myself to. There were no social prohibitions against staring; if something interested you, you looked at it, simple as that. How different from our culture, where an individual's privacy is valued above all, and staring is considered intrusive, even hostile behavior. Being an outsider, and an American at that, in such a small community made me an object of intense interest and scrutiny, and as such, people stared at me wherever I went. It was at these moments I realized how fully I was a product of my culture. Regardless of my perceived open-mindedness, I practically withered from this constant watch-fulness, this feeling that I was forever 'on-stage' performing like a circus animal for the public. So it was that I approached the miners, fidgeting as Maritsa made some introductory banter (most of which I still could not comprehend) and proceeded to introduce me one by one to all assembled.

One of the last people to make my acquaintance was a tall man with bulging eyes whom Maritsa told me was named Lyuben. He grinned as he shook my hand—engulfed it, really, as his palm was the size of a baseball glove and his fingers like relay batons—and

said something to Maritsa, which she translated back to me in her
Bulgarian-English hybrid: would I like to climb up the hill with
them to see how their job really worked? Looking up at the jagged,
rocky terrain, as severe and alien as the surface of the moon, I was
hesitant. I had no boots, only a pair of running sneakers, and
wore only a T-shirt and cargo shorts. Hardly the safest attire for
such a job. But as I looked around, I noticed most of the workers
were dressed little better, and I surmised (quite rightly, as it turned
out) that safety standards in Bulgaria were lax, if enforced at all.
Meanwhile, everyone continued to stare at me, awaiting a reply.
Part of the Peace Corps experience, it was reinforced again and
again, was diving headlong into a new culture and new
experiences, moving outside one's own comfort zone. With that in
mind, I shrugged and assented, earning a hearty round of
backslaps from all assembled.

Eventually, a man with a nineteenth-century mustache whom I
was told was the foreman (though no one bothered to introduce us)
stuck his head out the office door and announced that the shift had
started. Whatever humor and good spirits had existed in our little
group immediately vanished, and we started towards the foot of the
hill with the somber aspect of an infantry regiment marching
towards the front of an already doomed campaign.

What had seemed at a distance like a generally smooth rock
surface dotted at intervals by helpful outcroppings and footholds
turned out on closer inspection to be carpeted with loose dust and
pebbles that gave way beneath every footstep, sliding towards the
ground below like a miniature avalanche. One was forced to move
in short scrambles, hopping between the safety of boulders or
whatever solid anchor one could find to plant one's feet before
continuing on. I followed Lyuben's example, letting him map out a
trail for me that led to a leveled-off area about two-hundred feet
up where he had been digging for the last few weeks. I was about
halfway there when—turning for a moment to look down at

Maritsa, now a tiny version of herself so far away, like the center doll of a matryoshka—*I lost my footing and tumbled backwards, first sliding down the hillside on my back, my shirt and the skin underneath tearing from the friction, then managing to twist myself upright, mere seconds before my descent was cut short by a terrible impact that shook me to the core and left me on the brink of unconsciousness.*

In my cloudy mental state, I could hear people shouting, their voices garbled as if I were listening to them under water. Though I could not make out their words, their panic was evident, and while I knew their concern was directed toward me and that I had taken a nasty fall, I could not feel any pain and thought that any minute I would be able to shake off the cobwebs, stand up, and dust myself off. Those were the last thoughts I had before passing out. Only later, waking up in a hospital bed, would I find out my right leg had been shattered against the side of a boulder ...'

The first thing Charles became aware of were the blankets that covered him—not his own, nor like any he had ever felt before. The mattress, likewise, on which he slept was of an unfamiliar firmness, not the mattress from his basement room, nor the one from his childhood bed in his parents' home. This feeling of displacement, of helplessness, caused him to panic; a surge of adrenaline shot through him, dragging his mind back through the murky depths into full consciousness. He opened his eyes, blinked, and looked around the room.

Here was something familiar, though from where this familiarity sprung took a moment to sink in. The whitewashed walls and sterile plainness of the room struck a chord with him, but it was not until he had gathered the strength to lift his head and fully study his surroundings—the white-clad nurses, the IV standing over him, the polyester curtain separating him from the neighboring bed—that he realized he was in the hospital.

"How ya feeling?" said a voice next to him. He turned his head and saw his mother sitting in an armchair beneath the window, a magazine in her lap. "I was wondering when you'd wake up." She put the magazine down and slid her chair over to the side of the bed.

"I'm tired," said Charles, surprised at how hoarse and weak his voice sounded. "What happened? Why am I here?"

"You don't remember anything?"

Charles shook his head.

"You were down by the lake, walking along the boardwalk..."

"Yeah," said Charles, "that I remember."

"Do you remember falling off the pier onto the rocks?" she said.

Charles squinted at her. "What do you mean? I was reading on one of the benches."

"Yes, they did say they noticed you were reading a book."

"Who said?"

"The witnesses the police interviewed. They said they noticed you sitting on a bench, reading a book, when all of a sudden you stood up and started walking out along one of the piers. You were walking right along the edge trying to keep your balance, like you were on a tightrope or something. There was a boat docked out at the end, some small yacht. I don't know if you were trying to go out and look at it or what, but anyway, you lost your balance and fell off. I guess you hadn't made it too far, because you weren't even out over the water yet. You landed right on those big rocks at the edge of the shoreline."

Charles looked at her blankly. "I don't remember any of that."

His mother frowned. "I'll have to let the doctor know. Maybe you hit your head when you landed. How does your leg feel?"

"My leg? I don't feel anything."

"It's broken," she said. "In six places."

For the first time, Charles realized his leg was elevated in a sling, wrapped all the way up to his hip in a plaster cast.

"I didn't even notice," he said.

"The morphine must still be working. That's good, anyway." She sighed. "Oh Charlie, I wish I knew what was going on with you."

"That makes two of us." He reached up, slowly, and wiped some drool from the corner of his mouth. "How did you know I was here?"

"The receipt for your book. One of the paramedics saw my name was on it and gave it to the hospital so they could look me up and give me a call."

"Yeah, I was using it as a bookmark," said Charles.

She sighed and leaned forward to fix his blankets. "I have to leave soon. Do you need anything?"

"How long am I going to be here?"

"A while, yet. Maybe more than a month, so you better call work and let them know what happened. Or I can even call them for you if you want and tell them you won't—"

"I got fired."

"What?" She squinted, as though she'd misheard him.

"I was fired earlier today."

"Yesterday," she said. "You've been here overnight."

"That long?" His mother nodded. "Anyway, I showed up late," continued Charles. "I wasn't there to open the store, and they fired me."

"*Charlie...*" Her voice was full of disappointment, and she shook her head, looking off to her right as if she needed a second alone. When she turned to look at him again, her eyes were watery. She reached over and clasped his hand between both of hers. "What are you going to do when you get out of here?"

"I don't know." He looked at her sheepishly. "Come back with you, if I'm still allowed."

"Really? You mean it?"

"If you'll let me."

"Of *course* I will," she said, sniffling, a few joyful tears tracing a path down her cheek.

Soon after, she went home for the day, visiting hours having come to an end. Charles was left to drift in and out of a fitful, narcotized sleep, his dreams like a fog-shrouded version of his current reality: a hospital bed, an unfamiliar room, the patter of rain against his window, and out in the hallway, written on a door that led out to a courtyard, a word written in an unfamiliar language: "изход".

———————

Upon waking, Charles took a moment to scan his surroundings, preserved as though he had never moved away: the raised twin bed with the navy blue comforter; the oak dresser with brass handles in the corner; the wooden toy chest across the room where he kept his magazines, above which the faded yellow walls were chipped and cracked in a pattern that reminded him of the Niger River Delta. He remembered seeing a picture of it as a young boy—one of the first issues of *National Geographic* he had ever read—and from that point forward what had once been a random patch of peeling paint became forever a mysterious waterway halfway across the globe. There was no disassociating the images; they were inextricably linked in his mind. One became the other.

The sensation passed quickly, as it had every morning in the two weeks since he had left the hospital. All that remained was the reality of being at his parents' house. Pushing back the blankets, he swung his legs over the edge of the bed and sat up. His muscles, from his shoulders down to his feet, screamed in protest. The cast on his leg kept him immobilized throughout the night, making it impossible to roll over whenever he felt stiff. Sometimes this woke him up, leaving him dazed and groggy the following day; other times he was lucky enough to sleep through it, but paid for it later with a constant aching that wracked his body like arthritis. He stood up, grabbed his crutch from off the floor, and limped to the restroom, back bent and shivering, an elderly man at twenty-six.

Twenty-six years old, and nothing had changed; he was still a little boy. He had celebrated his birthday in the hospital, his mother the only guest to show up and the only one to bring him a present—a wool robe in a shiny silver box wrapped with a yellow ribbon. It was a nice gesture and a definite improvement—in warmth as well as dignity—on the paper-thin hospital gown he had been wearing up until then. His reaction, though, on opening the box and seeing what was inside, had been so indifferent that his mother was convinced he hated the gift, no matter how much he assured her it wasn't true. And it was not true—he did not hate the robe, recognized its practicality and understood what a thoughtful gesture it was. He simply did not have it in him to be moved by such things; he was as indifferent to receiving a gift as he was to the fact that no one else came to visit him in the hospital, that no one called or wrote to him to wish him happy birthday or to see how he was feeling. Though he understood these things as disappointments, he was neither angry nor sad that they had happened. They were simply facts that needed to be dealt with; emotions did not factor into it, anymore than they did into solving a math problem.

Charles shut the restroom door and tottered over to the toilet to pee. Leaning his crutch against the sink, he held onto the wall with one hand, while with the other he twisted and pulled at the waistband of his pajamas, slowly working them down around his plaster cast. When he had them down to his ankles, he moved his hand to the wall behind the toilet and leaned forward. His leg with the cast he pointed slightly back and out of the way, stretched out at an odd angle like a goalie making a kick save, before finally relieving himself. All the little tasks that made up daily life he had learned to do in this one-handed way.

He had learned his limits; making anything more than a simple microwave meal required too much movement and attention for half a body to handle, and so his mother took care of the cooking. Dropping something on the floor, if no one was around to fetch it for him, was enough to throw him into a fit of depression, requiring him to maneuver his body down into a sitting position to retrieve the item, then somehow keep it secured while he pulled himself, bit by bit, back into a standing position. These inconveniences were compounded by his father, who treated any request for assistance with the same sort of contempt he might treat a request for money, as if Charles had broken his leg on purpose in order to have his minor needs catered to.

Charles swung himself around to face the sink. He washed his hands and face, wrestled his pajamas back up, and, grabbing his crutch, hobbled out of the bathroom to the kitchen, where his father sat at the table reading the newspaper.

"Good morning," said Charles, as he entered the room.

His father raised his eyes for a second, and—seeing it was Charles—went right back to reading. "Morning," he said flatly.

"Good morning, sweetie," said his mother. She was standing by the stove off to his left, frying bacon in a pan. "You want some breakfast? This bacon's almost finished, and there's eggs, toast, coffee..." She scuttled over to the cupboard next to the refrigerator and looked inside. "There's also Pop-Tarts if you'd rather just have those. Or there's frozen waffles too, which I could make for you. It'll only take a minute."

Across the table, Charles's father sighed and noisily turned the page. Charles sat down opposite him and leaned his crutch against the table. "Just coffee for now," he said.

"Are you sure?" said his mother. "I don't want you getting hungry. We have potatoes. I could fry up some hash browns if you'd like."

"If he wants to eat, he'll eat," growled his father.

His mother, looking abashed, fell silent and went to pour Charles his coffee. She brought the cup over to him, along with a bottle of creamer, a carton of milk, and some sugar, so he could choose which he wanted. "Any plans for the day?" she asked.

"No," said Charles.

"I'm going grocery shopping later if you want to come with me."

"I don't know. I'll probably just be in the way."

"That's ridiculous!" she said.

Charles thought he heard his father snort under his breath. "I just mean with the crutch and the cast and everything," said Charles. "You know, those aisles are so narrow."

"How long until the cast comes off again?" said his father.

Charles sighed. "About a month, Dad."

"You know perfectly well how long, Elton," said his mother. "What the hell is wrong with you?"

"So you're just going to sit around reading for the next month?" said his father. "Can't even help your mother get groceries?"

"I don't *need* any help," she said. "I was just making the offer in case he felt like getting out of the house."

"Of course he doesn't want to get out of the house," said his father, turning the page noisily.

"What's that supposed to mean?" asked Charles.

His father folded up his paper and set it aside, practically rubbing his hands, as if he'd been biding his time until the opening for a fight arose. "What it means is that you seem perfectly happy to lay around all day with your nose stuck in a book while your mother and I take care of you."

"*You* take care of me?" said Charles. "When's the last time you did anything for me?"

"Look around you! Whose house do you think you're living in?" His father pointed a finger at his own chest. "That's my bed you're sleeping in, my TV you're watching, my food you're eating—all of it, mine."

"Excuse me," said his mother, "but last time I checked this house was *ours,* not yours. I still have some say in what goes on around here."

"What do you want me to do?" said Charles. His voice sounded weak, pleading, even to his own ears. "My leg is broken. There's nothing I can do about that."

"Right," said his father. "How did that happen again?"

Charles averted his gaze, turning to look out the window.

"Elton..." said his mother.

"You fell off the side of a dock," Charles's father answered. "You were sitting on a bench, you stood up, you walked out along the edge of a dock, and fell right off onto the rocks." He shook his head in disbelief. "Even for you, that's pretty pathetic."

Charles squirmed in his seat, unable to look at his father, unable to mount any kind of defense. There was nothing he could say because he remembered nothing, only a seamless transition from sitting down to read to waking up in the hospital, his leg in a cast. Claiming amnesia sounded even worse to him than just keeping silent, accepting his father's abuse until he could excuse himself and retreat to the safety of his room.

"And so what now?" asked his father. "What are you going to do when that leg heals and you have no more reason to lay around here letting your mother take care of you?"

"He's going back to school!" cried his mother, almost like a plea to leave her son alone.

Charles had never said anything about enrolling in school, but he didn't dare contradict her. He knew quite well she was all he had left.

"Then why isn't he online looking at colleges? Why isn't he looking for a job to pay for books and tuition? Or don't you think it's enough we give him food and clothes and a place to lay around and be a deadbeat? We're supposed to pay for his school too?"

"Charles," said his mother. Her voice was anxious and coaxing, the way one might speak to an animal when imploring it to do a trick for one's guests. "Have you given any thought to where you might like to go to grad school?"

Before he could formulate a suitable lie, his father broke in. "He's not going to school. Even community college wouldn't take him. Not that he could afford it if they did. He slacked his way through high school, he slacked his way through college, and now he's slacking his way through life. It's time you faced up to it, Janine—our son is a nobody, and he'll always be a nobody."

"No, Ma," said Charles, unable to look either of his parents in the eyes, "I haven't decided yet."

"Decide nothing," said his father. "I'll tell you what you can decide—where you're going to move when your leg is better. Because the second you can stand on your own you're walking right out this door. There are plenty of apartment listings online. I suggest you start looking ASAP. And fill out some job applications while you're at it. No one's going to rent to you if you don't have work."

Charles looked to his mother for support, but she only shrugged and arched her eyebrows, as if to say, "There's nothing more I can do for you."

They stood that way for a few moments, staring at one another in silence, until Charles's father, realizing he had won, clapped his hands and said, "Well, I'm gonna run to the mall for a few minutes, and then I'm headed over to Gary's to watch the game. When I get back, you can show me all the information you spent the day printing off the computer, and we'll decide where to go from there." And with that, he put on his shoes and was out the door.

When it was just Charles and his mother, he pleaded for her to intercede on his behalf, but she would hear none of it.

"Honestly, Charles, I don't know what you expect," she said. For the first time, he heard exasperation creeping into her voice. "When I first told you I wanted you to move back, there was always the expectation that you would use the opportunity to make something better for yourself. I understand you're in pain and need to recover, but even I get the feeling sometimes you're not interested in doing anything more than just getting by. Your father . . . "

"My father hates me," said Charles, gazing at the floor.

"Enough," said his mother. "Enough with the self-pity. I know your father can be rude, even cruel sometimes. But he's letting you stay here. That's not hate, Charles, believe me. His patience might be worn thin, but that's only because he cares and expects bigger things out of you."

Charles had heard this flaccid apology-cum-lecture from his mother more times than he could remember. In the beginning—as a young boy, before he knew better—it had always succeeded in shaming him. Even now, untold years and recitations later, it still gave him pause, this idea that somewhere deep down his father believed in him, possibly even loved him. It was one of the central fictions that had sustained him all these years, no matter how bad his life became.

"I'm going," he said, and started limping off toward his room.

"Where?" said his mother. Charles could hear in her voice that she wanted him to stay, but he did not stop.

"To read."

He did not hear what she said next; she did not follow him, and he made no effort to go back to her. When he reached his room he turned around—half-hopping, leaning on his crutch—and shut and locked the door behind him. Then he went over to the nightstand and switched on the lamp, its claustrophobic, orange glow spreading through the room like a sickness. Sitting down and sliding back on the mattress, he groped around under his pillow until he felt the familiar contours and textured pages he loved so much. Pulling out his book, looking down at its green-and-gray cover, he began to regret walking away from his mother like that, from the one who had done so much for him when everyone else had moved on and abandoned him.

He was on the verge of getting up again, going back out to the living room and asking her forgiveness, but the pull of the book was just too much, only the slightest coaxing from his thumb necessary to open up onto a world so far from the one in which he toiled each day. Right up until the last second, when he finally succumbed to temptation, he was convinced he would put the book aside, stand up, and repair the damage he had done. Right up until the last second, when he laid eyes on the tiny rows of print, and his consciousness dissipated like a fog rising toward the peaks of the *Stara Planina* ...

'A habit started around the office of ditching work at midday and dining at a nearby mehana *called "Sekvoya," our lunch hour extending late into the night as we drank ourselves over the moon with rakia and vodka. The mayor himself spearheaded this initiative, and so absolutely no one had any reservations about letting loose. It was as if some grand bacchanalian spirit had seized the whole building and reduced our restraint and judgment to that of a fraternity house. Even the plainest, most sexless middle-aged receptionist would be red-faced by three, falling over*

giggling by six, and hanging off the neck of an equally besotted clerk by eight, when the TVs were turned off and the radio turned up, blaring the Serbian pop music the mayor loved so much.

Being only a few months into my stay at Zemen I was still regarded as a guest, and consequently was the target of frequent entreaties to drink, as well as the subject of numerous toasts as florid and gushing as Shakespearean sonnets. The only thing not tolerated at these get-togethers was the sight of me without a drink in my hand, and no sooner had I choked down one glass of grape brandy than another appeared before me, someone at the table bellowing "nazdrave!" so that I had no choice but to dive back in.

In the beginning I was amazed by the speed with which I became intoxicated, by late afternoon already groping my way to the restroom while my colleagues sat at the table pleasantly chatting with the clear eyes and easy composure of lifelong teetotalers. No doubt I was familiar with the clichés about the Slavic people, their seeming invulnerability to vodka and cold (not to mention their unrelenting grimness, a sort of terminal pessimism that made "every birthday a funeral," as one of my Bulgarian friends once put it. But that's a subject for another discussion). I was far from a novice when it came to alcohol—after my parents threw me out of the house, my leg barely mended, it was my constant companion for months—and I could not make sense of a ninety-pound waif matching me shot for shot being able to strut across the dance floor in stiletto heels, while I could barely muster the coordination to get out of my chair.

Instead of focusing on my food and drink, I began to study my companions, to see what it was that differentiated us. That was when I became aware how contrasting the Bulgarian and American eating styles were. While I was busy wolfing down my shopska salata *and* ezik purzhen, *my co-workers were engaged in a ritual of monastic restraint, taking single bites of their meal, then setting down their fork (upside-down, tines resting on the edge of the plate) and talking, or even just staring at one another, sometimes for up to twenty minutes, without taking another bite. For all the toasts and importance placed on drinking, I never saw anyone take more than the most miniscule sip, whereas I—being raised in a country where drinking is a primary rather than supplemental activity—had been gulping away with impunity. It was also around that time I learned about other Bulgarian peculiarities such as indirect communication, gossip and the lack of recognition of an individual's privacy. When one day Vyara, a young girl with whom I was friendly, went out of her way to avoid me at work, I went to Maritsa's office and asked her if something was wrong.*

"She's embarrassed," said Maritsa.

"Of what?" I asked.

"Of you. She thinks you have a drinking problem."

"A drinking problem? She was the one who kept pushing me to drink all last night!"

It was true. All throughout the previous evening, Vyara had followed me around the room with a bottle of Savoy Silver Club, my own personal valet, topping off my glass before it was even half empty and thwarting any attempt to pause with a forceful "haide!", while miming putting a glass to her mouth.

"She was just being polite," said Maritsa.

"I told her 'no thank you' a million times!"

Maritsa nodded, lips pressed together. "She knew that you were just being polite."

"Why didn't she say something, if she was so worried?"

"She did. She asked you if you were enjoying the music."

"So?"

"So if you enjoyed the music, it only made sense that you should dance, and if you danced, then you would have to put down your glass and stop drinking."

"But I didn't enjoy the music."

"You don't like Lili Ivanova!?!"

Such were the perplexing rules of social life in small-town Bulgaria. Another consequence of being a young, single, American male was that it was taken for granted I should be paired with a young, single Bulgarian female at the soonest possible instance, a burden that the entire adult population of Zemen took upon itself with a sort of patriotic fervor. There was, I was told, nothing comparable in beauty or virtue to the Bulgarian woman.

On the few weekend excursions I had made to Sofia, the capital, nothing I saw disabused me of this notion. Up and down Vitosha Boulevard, in front of boutiques selling three-hundred-dollar sweaters and five-hundred-dollar "designer" jeans, paraded a bevy of long-legged, thick-lipped, perky-breasted angels, as if the street were one long Victoria's Secret runway. Despite the long tradition of American men scoring out of their league in foreign countries—or perhaps because of it—I was reluctant to approach these budding goddesses, intimidated by their looks and haughty expressions, and also afraid that any interest they did show would be predicated on money or my ability to get them a green card. Only later did I learn how much I had shortchanged these girls, how much broader and fuller their lives were than the myopic desire to escape abroad (though the desire certainly did exist).

In the villages, though, things were different. There were girls in Zemen every bit as attractive as those in Sofia, at least at first glance. If one looked closely, however, one began to notice subtle differences. There was a certain weathered aspect to their good looks, a beaten-down quality that lay just below the surface and against which their youth acted as a temporary bulwark. In the stunning, sensual girl of twenty, with her porcelain skin, statuesque figure and long, silky mane, one could already glimpse the wrinkled, sagging, scarred and flea-bitten woman of thirty, as if in those ten years she would age fifty. Still, these were the girls, my colleagues told me, that I wanted for a wife. "All those Sofia girls want to do is go out dancing and drinking in clubs," went a familiar refrain. "They don't know the first thing about cooking or cleaning." Village girls—"real" Bulgarian girls—I was told, would be true to the end. Always would there be a delicious meal waiting for me when I got home from work, always would the house be spotless, and always, it was hinted, would my needs be met in the bedroom.

Perhaps because of all the time we spent there, the first choice deemed to be a suitable mate for me was a waitress at Sekvoya named Stanislava. Not a single instance passed, when Stanislava would bring us another round of meze or refill our drinks, without someone at the table loudly asking me if I found her beautiful, or asking her whether she would like to kiss me, or even ordering her to sit for a moment in one of the seats next to mine so that we could become acquainted, while everyone stopped what they were doing to watch us, like we were dancing bears. For a country so dependent on indirect communication, there was shockingly little decorum when it came to discussing my love life.

"Stanislava, eh?" said Ivo, the mayor's driver, one evening at the café. "Vroom, vroom!" he blurted, pumping his arms as he thrust his hips back and forth. It was as if I had traveled to the other side of the planet and discovered my old junior high school. Stanislava was barely out of school herself, eighteen years old, with all the youthful, coltish beauty that entailed.

For all their indelicateness, part of me secretly encouraged my colleagues' efforts to bring Stanislava and me together. Her body turned the head of every man (and even some women) each and every time she walked across the dining room. Her enormous breasts were on the constant verge of escape from the baby-blue ribbed sweater she wore as a uniform, and into which she had cut her own plunging, "V"-shaped neckline with a pair of scissors.

The black tights she wore rode so low they had to cling to her hipbones to keep from falling, like a mountain climber dangling from a precipice by his fingertips, as her backside twitched to and fro, doing its own private kyuchek *to the rhythm of Serbian turbo-folk.*

Still, the signs of wear I had mentioned were clearly visible— the swollen, sagging eyes, already surrounded by tiny cracks and wrinkles, and the look of perpetual exhaustion; the crooked teeth, stained from years of coffee and cigarettes; the wild, untamed eyebrows and hint of mustache along the upper lip. They were the byproducts of poverty, and I believe it is in the faces of the young women of Bulgaria that one can really begin to understand just how hard life there can be. The pessimism that seems to be their national birthright not only resides in their hearts but is written on their skin.

Nevertheless, despair had yet to completely claim Stanislava, and I was bewitched by her reserved manner—so out of context with the clothes she wore—and the way she blushed and drew into herself whenever my colleagues began trying to push us together. Though their pointed, personal questions made me uncomfortable too, I was also a little worried about Stanislava's reaction. Was she so embarrassed because she didn't find me attractive, I wondered?

My fears were allayed the first time I saw Stanislava on the street. I was on my way to a magazin *to buy batteries for my camera when I saw her coming the other way, barely recognizing her at first out of her restaurant uniform. She wore a brown corduroy jacket and jeans, and as we got close she flashed me a gap-toothed grin and said, "Zdrasti, Charley" in her husky smoker's voice. Her eyes batted coquettishly at me, and I stared in dumb adoration as she walked past. Before turning the corner, she gave one last glance over her shoulder to see if I was still watching her.*

From that day on we were inseparable. I got her address from Maritsa, who had spread word around the office that I had finally gotten the hint and was going to Stanislava to ask for her hand. All their efforts had paid off, she told my co-workers, and as I left the obshtina *everyone came out of their offices to congratulate me and lay claim to their wedding invitation. Though I did my best to disabuse them of this notion, reminding them we hadn't even had our first date yet, they assured me it hardly mattered and that marriage was inevitable. I hurried outside and found Donka the gypsy, who sold roses in the restaurants around the town center, bought a dozen flowers from her, and took them to Stanislava's house.*

Her mother was baffled to find an American man on her doorstep bearing a bright-red bouquet, having never met me before and only vaguely aware that an Amerikanets *was in town doing some kind of volunteer work. I asked in broken Bulgarian if her daughter was home, and after disappearing into the other room, she returned a few moments later pushing Stanislava in front of her, gripping her by the shoulders as if she were a stubborn animal who might wander off in another direction if left untended.*

*"*K'vo stava?*" said Stanislava, confused, trying to squirm loose from her mother's grasp. Then she caught sight of me standing in the doorway and stopped, her cheeks going red as two stop signs as she stammered hello. Mustering all the courage and vocabulary I had, I explained to her mother my intention to ask her daughter on a date and asked if I might have her permission. I know it sounds terribly old-fashioned, and I'm not even sure if it's common practice in Bulgaria, but it felt like the right thing to do in the moment. Stanislava's mother seemed pleased. If Stani wanted to go, she had no problem with it, she told me. "*Kude shte otidem?*" Stani asked me. Where could we go in Zemen? I told her I would take her to Sofia for the day, my treat. It hardly seemed extravagant in my mind, but the way her eyes lit up you would have thought I was taking her to Paris.*

That Saturday, we met at the train station and rode into the capital. In the morning we strolled past Alexander Nevsky and the antique market, then lunched at Ugo *in the Five Corners and spent the afternoon browsing the book bazaar and window shopping along Vitosha Boulevard. With a few hours to kill before our train left for Zemen, we sat on the benches in front of Ivan Vazov Theater and watched the old men playing chess. There, as the sun went down over the park, we shared our first kiss.*

It's been two months since that day, and I can truly say that I'm in love. Sorry to gush on about this stuff, but I think girls are a more sympathetic audience for this kind of thing. It's not really something you can talk to other guys about. Anyway, I hope everything is going just as good for you in California. If you ever get tired of the movie business, there's always room for you out here in the rest of the world. It's really amazing, starting over. I'm glad I took your advice. Now I owe you one.

Hopefully I hear back from you soon. I've been worried my letters aren't finding their way through to you, in which case this has all been one giant exercise in futility. The postal system in Bulgaria is not always as reliable as in the States, so there's no way to tell when and if this will reach your mailbox. But if you are reading this, my address is at the bottom of the page. Drop me a line whenever you get the chance (I know you're really busy). Even thousands of miles away, I still think about you all the time and hope you're happy in life. Take care. Dovizhdane za sega...

Iskreno tvoi,
Charles

When Jasmine finished the letter she turned it over several times, as if looking for a clue she had missed, before opening her nightstand and adding it to the top of the pile inside. It was the fourth letter she had received that month. Each one had left her more unsettled. A thought occurred to her, and she checked the envelope in which the letter had come—the postmark was from

Pennsylvania. There were no stamps or marks anywhere showing it had been mailed from Bulgaria. On a whim, she tried dialing his cell number again, but as on previous attempts found only a recording telling her the number was no longer in service. She went online and searched for a database of Peace Corps volunteers, but could not find his name listed anywhere.

It became a minor obsession for her, trying to make heads or tails of what had happened to that nice guy from high school whom she had befriended one fall, the year Auntie died, but eventually, his letters to her became less and less frequent. Soon she stopped hearing from him altogether. She got a new job with a different studio, met someone and moved into a new apartment, during which all the old letters were thrown out with the trash. Some time later she got engaged, and—immersed in work and planning her wedding—no longer spared a thought for Charles, whose image slipped from her memory like a dream upon waking.

Stories

My Second Major Breakup

She said she'd met a violin-maker from Italy and had fallen madly in love. This hardly seemed likely. He had told her his shop was just down the street from where Stradivarius had apprenticed as a young man. I asked her what part of Italy, and she froze. "Cremona," she said, after a minute. Well, that much was right. Maybe she was telling the truth after all.

My ancestors came from Italy, I reminded her. The ones on my mother's side, anyway. From Belluna, in the north. Not far from Cremona. Very famous for its sunglasses. Right now, I said, a second cousin of mine is probably designing for Fendi. I could get her a discount.

But it was no use—violins had won her heart. Materialism trumped by romanticism, modernism by Old-World charm. I appealed to her practical side. Italian men are sleazy, I told her. They're in love with their mothers and never mature. They catcall and grope and chain-smoke unfiltered cigarettes. "None of them drive cars," I said. "They all zip around on scooters. You know how bad your balance is. You'll never make it there."

"I'll just hold on to Paolo and let him drive," she said. Nothing would sway her; she had it all figured out. While Paolo worked in his studio, she would clean their apartment and do the shopping. When he returned home in the evening, a piping-hot meal would be waiting for him on the table. Pretty domesticated stuff for a one-time feminist. She replied that feminism had many guises. A very convenient ideology. In her spare time she planned on visiting the countryside and doing a little painting. *Painting.* It was like talking to someone with Stockholm syndrome.

My ammunition grew thinner. I fell back on the practicalities of the matter—the difficulty of obtaining a visa, the cost of uprooting and moving across the ocean. "What's bureaucracy in the face of love?" she said. I rolled my eyes and offered to help her pack.

She moved out on a Sunday morning, two big bags under her arms. Down by the curb she dropped them and waited with hands on hips, looking up and down the street while I watched from the window above. A silver sedan pulled up and she loaded the bags into the trunk. I couldn't tell if it was Paolo; no one got of the car to help her. *Fine beginning*, I thought. As she went around to the passenger's side, stepping up onto the sidewalk, the heel of her shoe snapped off and made her stumble; I could hear her cursing as she limped over to the car, got inside and slammed the door. The cobblestone of Cremona would not be kind to her.

The Haberdasher

Nigel Moon wasn't sure how the haberdasher had gotten into his room. Indeed, the events leading up to that moment were conspicuously absent from his memory. The last thing he remembered was walking home from the carnival, bathed in a late-July sweat, thrilled at his success only a few hours earlier in acquiring a large, stuffed tortoise for a girl named Fiona Kleinschmidt. This had required Moon to break three successive balloons with a set of darts, a task he performed expertly and with some measure of panache, judging by the annoyed reaction of the attending carny. "All right, bub," he had growled. "Here's your prize. Take it and get lost." Fiona and Moon had giggled, totally indifferent in that way unique to the young and in-love, and sped off arm in arm.

"The funny thing about this," said Moon at last, "is that I'm not even sure what a haberdasher is."

"A haberdasher deals in men's wares," said the man, gesturing around the room. "As you can plainly see."

Indeed, scattered across the floor, the windowsill and the foot of the bed were an array of jackets, vests and elegant dress shirts, along with a sewing kit, measuring tape and other tools typical of a clothier.

"I know what you're thinking," said the haberdasher. "*But I thought a haberdasher dealt solely with buttons, ribbons, zippers and the like.* Well, strictly speaking, in the traditional, English sense of the word, you'd be right. But in America the definition has been expanded to encompass all aspects of a men's outfitter. Your confusion is understandable."

Moon had been thinking nothing of the sort. His confusion had much more to do with the man standing in front of him and how he had gained access to Moon's apartment. Had Moon himself invited him in? That was highly unlikely, considering Moon was in bed, still dressed in pajamas. Clearly the haberdasher had broken into his apartment. That made him a criminal; Moon wondered if he was supposed to be nervous. He didn't feel nervous. Should he call the cops?

"Should I call the cops?" asked Moon.

"Don't be silly," said the haberdasher. "There's no time for that. We've got to get you fitted."

"Fitted? For what?"

The haberdasher sighed. "That's three questions in less than ten seconds. At this rate we don't stand a chance."

"A chance at what?"

Moon blushed, realizing he had just asked another question. Then he became furious at blushing; this was, after all, his house, his bedroom, which some mysterious man had broken into, replete with garments, and if he—that's Moon—wanted to ask questions, that damn well seemed reasonable to him—again, Moon.

"Yeah, that's right," said Moon, in response to a look from the haberdasher, "and I'm going to keep on asking until I get some answers. You haven't been straight with me once since you showed up. Who are you, anyway? Why are you here?"

"All right," said the haberdasher, sighing again, "I can see this is going to have to run its course. As I said before, I am here to measure you and fit you for a tuxedo. My name is Needlebaum; I wouldn't have thought it necessary to tell you that, being that you hired me, personally, to come here today."

"I hired you?" Moon winced—*another question*.

"Yes, and paid me a handsome sum. Really, I find this all perplexing. On the eve of the biggest day of your life you're acting positively batty, obsessing over trifles instead of letting me do my job. Unless . . . " Needlebaum drew in a sharp breath. "You're getting cold feet, aren't you?"

"Cold feet?"

"It's understandable, I suppose. Not all that uncommon. Most people wonder if they're doing the right thing when the moment finally arrives. But really, sir, if my advice means anything to you, then do whatever you need to do—have a stiff drink, take a walk, et cetera—to put your fears aside. But do it in the next twenty or thirty minutes. I can't stress enough how short on time we are. And really, sir, it's all inevitable at this point anyway. Best to face it in stride."

Moon felt as though he was floating on air. It was all he could do to keep reminding himself that *he* was the one in charge, that it was *his* house this haberdasher had barged into and that *he* was the one who would dictate when and how things got done. He sat up in bed, feeling this might give him a confidence and air of authority that had been missing up to this point.

"Exactly how much did I pay you?" asked Moon.

"Ah ha ha!" said Needlebaum. "As sir is no doubt aware, I find it unseemly to discuss the financial particulars of a business transaction openly with the customer. Good grace and etiquette demand a certain amount of discretion. Perhaps the only thing my humble profession shares in common with the world's oldest. In terms of emotional connection, however, they are in sharp contrast. Never doubt for a moment that I have your best interests at heart. Which is why," he said, glancing at his watch, "we really must be moving along."

Moon knew what the haberdasher was doing. Having spent two of his college years as a certified Cutco representative, he was intimately acquainted with the 'hard sell'. Relentless pressure—he had once convinced a housewife her very marriage was on the brink of collapse due to the shoddy cuts of meat she served for dinner, torn and mangled by her substandard kitchen knives. He sold two deluxe sets of Cutco cutlery that day, shedding a little of his dignity in the process. But with each new bout of self-debasing, a cynical, world-weary wisdom had developed that made him a difficult mark. The more Needlebaum pressed him, the more Moon resolved to take his time, effect a casual approach to induce frustration. Once Needlebaum was rattled he would be much more likely to slip up and reveal potentially useful information.

"So what happens if I listen to you and let you measure me?" asked Moon.

"Chiefly," said Needlebaum, "you will acquire a new tuxedo. One which fits properly, I should add."

"And what do I need with a new tuxedo?"

"You would look pretty silly turning up like that."

"My pajamas? Obviously I intend on getting dressed first."

"T-shirts and jeans would not be appropriate."

"No problem. I can throw on a shirt and tie from the office."

Moon detected the slightest hint of red in the haberdasher's face. His tactic was working.

"Sir, I really must protest."

"Protest!?!" bellowed Moon. This was the next phase—unmitigated rage. Now that Needlebaum had his dander up it was time to shout him down, keep him off balance. It was a technique the more savvy of Moon's customers had used against him, and was the only really effective way to rid oneself of a tenacious salesman. "Who's the customer here!?! Who paid who a large sum of money...!?!"

"Who paid *whom*, sir."

"I paid you, you twit! And I don't remember requesting grammar lessons. Or is that a complimentary service?" Moon sprang out of bed and opened the bedroom door. "Good day," he said, gesturing outside.

"Sir?"

"Get out. I'm cancelling my order."

Needlebaum's face remained impassive, but Moon could see the sudden tenseness in his arms and legs, hear the unevenness of his breathing. Moon's threat had deeply shaken him. Now was the time to soften the blow, draw him back in with a gesture of friendship.

"Naturally, I understand the inconvenience of cancelling at such a late hour. Whatever sort of fee you charge is perfectly acceptable. Just deduct it from my ... "

Moon froze in midsentence. He barely had time to register the plump, middle-aged man springing toward him like a cat before a hand clamped itself over his mouth. In it was a rag, doused in a noxious chemical that made Moon gag. Moon felt his body go limp. His legs gave way and he crumpled to the floor. The more he struggled, the tighter the haberdasher's grip became; Moon inhaled the acrid fumes, feeling his eyelids grow heavy. He knew that if his eyes closed he would lose consciousness for good.

Moon was on his stomach now, the haberdasher on top of him. Unable to move, he tried everything he could to stay awake—biting his lip, digging his nails deep into his skin—but he knew it was too late. Just off to his left, Moon spied an umbrella lying on the floor. Slowly he worked his left arm free, continuing to struggle against the haberdasher to keep him distracted. Sliding his hand along the floor, he stretched out towards the umbrella's handle. His fingertips grazed the wood. Just a few more inches and he would have it.

Moon opened his eyes. After a few minutes he realized was lying on his back on top of the bed. He tried to sit up and immediately fell back; his head reeled, buffeted by waves of nausea. He felt his breath, heavy and throbbing, in the back of his throat. Moon's eyes scanned the room; there was no sign of the haberdasher anywhere, but something draped across the chair in the corner caught his attention. It seemed to shine, like it was made of metal. Struggling up onto his elbows, Moon craned his neck to get a closer look. He saw that it was not metal at all, but a sheet of plastic, reflecting the light. Inside the plastic was something black. Fighting back the discomfort, Moon dragged himself to the edge of the bed and lurched to his feet. Going over to the chair, he tore open the plastic and held up the object inside—a new tuxedo. Pinned to the breast was an invoice slip; Moon was dismayed to learn returns were not accepted.

The Inquisitor

She was fifty, but looked thirty-five. Black cocktail dress, silver bracelet, dark eyes and diamond pendant dangling from a chain around her neck. Hair, also dark, trimmed into a bob that fell just below her slender jawline. Hands clasped below her waist, she glided through the open doorway and stood in front of Klein's desk. Around her shoulders was a silk scarf, which she removed and let fall onto one of the chairs lined against the wall.

Klein stood up. "Please raise your right hand," he said. The woman did so. "Do you swear that your answers will be the truth, the whole truth and nothing but the truth?"

"I do swear it," she said, letting slip a grin.

Klein frowned. "Please, have a seat." While the woman made herself comfortable, he gave a cursory glance at her file. "My name is Officer Klein, Ms. Patel. If you don't mind, we're going to start off with the reading and writing exam, and from there we'll move on to civics."

What amazed Klein, only six months into his job as an interviewing officer, was how repetitive were the tasks he performed. One of the things that had appealed to him when he had accepted the position was the variety it had seemed to promise, the chance to interact with people from every corner of the globe and to learn about their disparate lives.

"Now, Ms. Patel, I'm going to have you write a sentence for me—"

"Oh, please," she said, "call me Indra. I can't stand formalities. They make me feel old."

"Indra, then." Klein pointed to the worksheet on the table in front of her. "Right here on line number one, I need you to write, 'He went to the post office.'"

How many times in the last six months had he asked someone to write this sentence? More than he could remember. On his first day of work he had been given a list with more than fifty sentences the federal government had deemed appropriate for testing applicants' ability to write in English. But nearly every time, Klein settled on, "He went to the post office." And it wasn't just him; nearly all officers, he had come to find out, developed a favorite sentence at some point in their career. Klein's friend, Malreaux, who had started around the same time as Klein, preferred, "You drink too much coffee." He found it amusing the way it passed judgment on his applicants' habits while simultaneously testing their writing skills.

Klein wasn't sure what had drawn him to his particular sentence, but he was amazed at the myriad ways he had seen it written. Often, if there were any mistake at all, it was a simple misspelling—an "s" instead of a "c" in "office", or the word "want" instead of "went". But every once in a while a strange and wonderful gem would surface—Klein remembered with particular fondness a Tunisian man who had written, without a moment's hesitation, "She winks at the pork sausage"—that had filled his heart with gratitude, even as he was forced to administer a failing grade.

Ms. Patel made no such errors. Her pen moved across the paper in long, elegant sweeps, and when she reached the denouement and had added the final punctuation, she looked up from the desk and announced breathlessly, "Finished!"

Klein pointed farther down the page. "And now if you can read this paragraph for me."

Ms. Patel cleared her throat. "The teacher spoke to the class before the party began," she recited. Her accent had an affected Englishness about it, a sort of generic, bourgeoisie inflection he had encountered before on the rare occasions he ventured to the Upper East Side. Yet on certain words a hint of her native Indian accent slipped through, try as she might to suppress it.

Klein was embarrassed to admit he couldn't remember how the rest of the paragraph went. He had read it once and found the content crudely jingoistic. Silly, inserting propaganda into a process designed to test a person's ability to read. He stared at the wall and waited for her to finish.

After that came the civics test, ten random questions about America and its government, a nation's essence reduced to a series of numbers—13 stripes, 50 states, 100 senators, 435 representatives. Ms. Patel answered the first six questions correctly. "Okay," said Klein. "That's it. We can stop."

"I pass?"

"You pass."

"Oh, thank you!" She reached below her seat, where her purse was, and took out a paper fan, which she unfolded and waved back and forth in front of her face.

"I can't tell you how nervous I was. That's why I involve myself with the arts," she said. "Anything having to do with tests, and my mind just freezes up. I'm terrified of them."

Klein smiled politely and let the comment pass. Artists, in his experience, loved to talk about themselves and their work. If he acknowledged her comment there was no telling how long she might go on; already he saw little chance of completing the interview in the allotted twenty minutes.

His plan bore fruit. She abruptly fell silent, speaking again only when he asked a direct question. "Now, Ms. Patel—"

"Indra," she said.

"I'm sorry, Indra. Can I see your green card and passport?" Klein reached out to receive the documents. "And your Social Security card, if you have it. I just need to make sure everything matches what's written on your form."

"Here you are," she said, handing over the requested items. Her hand remained on the desk next to Klein's as he checked over the documents.

"Can you tell me your date of birth?" he asked her.

"November 10, 1959."

"And have you ever been married?"

"I was married once," she said airily.

"You're divorced?"

"I prefer to think of myself as free." She waved a hand as if sweeping away the past. "Once was enough. Never again!"

Klein smiled. "Never say never."

"Dear, when you're as old as I am, "never" isn't such a long time."

"You aren't so old."

"Fifty?"

"You don't look fifty."

"Ah, you see?" Indra leaned back in her chair and crossed her legs. "If I were younger I would fall for a line like that. No, I'll never settle down. I'm in love with New York. If New York were a man, I would marry him. London is where I grew up, but I've lived in New York for almost twenty years now. My studio is in New York. It inspires me."

"Yes, your studio," said Klein. "You're self-employed then?"

"I am." She leaned forward again, across the table. "It's more of a gallery than a studio, per se, but I do use a section of it as a workshop for my own ideas. Wait..." She reached down into her bag again and took out her wallet. "Take one of these," she said, handing him a business card. "It has the address and phone number of the studio. You should come by sometime. I'm there all the time. Day or night."

"I'll add it to the file," said Klein, as he took the card from her. But Indra held onto his hand, turning it to examine the white-gold band on his ring finger.

"You're married," she said.

Klein jerked his hand loose. "Ms. Patel, we need to stick to your application."

He kept his eyes on her file, but from the few glances he sneaked of her face, it was clear she was embarrassed.

The rest of the interview went quickly, but there existed now a tension between them. Inexplicably, Klein mourned this change. It pained him that for the rest of her life this woman would look back on him and find only the memory of a cold, officious man, someone whose company it had been necessary to tolerate rather than enjoy. Perhaps he could rebuild the bridge, he thought, but a glance at the clock dashed all hope. Once more, he was behind.

In the end he was able to approve the woman, which he supposed was some sort of consolation. But he felt a sudden hostility toward her as he shook her hand and led her from the office.

As they approached the final hallway, Klein bid her good-bye and pointed the way to the exit. As she glided away from him, growing more and more distant, Klein was startled to hear himself calling after her to come back. But his voice had grown weak, and she would not turn around, not even to wave good-bye.

Appearance and Coincidence

A gale wind blew across the city, and Oakridge McWillams lost his top hat.

With many a dip and flutter, it raced down Hobart Street, past townhouses stacked tall and tight like books on a shelf, like one of those hoops children in olden times used to push for fun.

McWilliams had a friend, Frau M, who lived on the corner where Hobart crossed paths with Bettencourt Lane. Stepping out on her porch, she caught sight of the top hat flopping and rolling past her front walk into the street beyond. Had she recognized to whom it belonged (for McWilliams had only purchased it recently, and wore it sparingly), she almost surely would have dashed to the sidewalk and attempted to retrieve it. Such was her nature. But in truth, it was already too late. Frau M watched helplessly as the hat disappeared, crushed beneath the tires of a passing motorbus.

Or so it appeared from Frau M's vantage point. With the hat gone, her attention returned to the front walk, where a panting Oakridge McWilliams now appeared.

He skidded to a halt in front of her gate, impeded from further progress by the bus, which was unloading a line of passengers onto the curb. His face was all dismay; Mrs. Wentleworth, the baker, whose vocabulary ran more colorful than Frau M's, would have described him as "having a puss on."

"Mr. McWilliams," said Frau M, who insisted on a certain level of formality, even with close acquaintances, "you appear agitated."

McWilliams—doubled over, hands on knees, his chest heaving—attempted to straighten himself, began to answer, stopped, raised his finger, continued heaving, opened his mouth, choked slightly and coughed, before doubling over once more, hands again on knees.

"Your face is flush," continued Frau M, "and some sweat has beaded up near your temple. There! It's beginning to trickle down past your ear."

Frau M was German, though she had not set foot in Germany since the age of twelve. It was due to her excessive formality that people referred to her as "Frau"; on her arrival, she had continually introduced herself as "Frau M", and the people of her neighborhood—being sharp-minded in a way that encompassed no knowledge of the outside world, and discarding formalities as a rule—mistook it to be her first name.

"Frau..." said McWilliams, at last finding his voice, "I've lost my hat."

"Your hat? Was it a top hat, by chance? Black wool, with what appeared to be a grosgrain ribbon ending in a side bow?"

"Yes, that's the one!"

"I believe it's beneath the tires of this bus."

McWilliams let out a moan and looked on as the bus, unburdened of its passengers, pulled away, expecting to see the mangled remains of his favorite accessory ground into the pavement. But there appeared only an empty space, leaving him and Frau M to wonder.

Descending his front steps, Somerset Windgap felt the wind slicing through him like a thousand icy darts, and thought better of leaving the house ungloved. Slight of frame and with a wan complexion, he possessed not the fortitude to bear Nature's brunt.

Reappearing on his porch, hands and neck now shrouded in wool, he began his walk to the chemist's. It was a walk he had made often, and normally, nothing—from the lilac-filled flower boxes below Mrs. Lycoming's picture window to the blood-red maple whose branches Mr. Kilbuck had allowed to encroach on the sidewalk near the corner of Glenwood Avenue—commanded his attention. So it was with some considerable shock that near the aforementioned corner, Somerset Windgap found a top hat sitting where none should appear.

For as long as he could remember, Windgap had had an affinity for maps. To a man with no money, like himself, they were an invitation to daydream, a coded message in a long-forgotten language calling one to boldness. It was customary, whenever he gazed at a map, to imagine himself a tiny cursor moving over the landscape, climbing mountain ranges and skirting bodies of water with strange names that managed to trip his tongue even in his imagination. As he meandered from country to country, city to city, even between neighborhoods (such was his mania for all maps), a montage played in the background, still images—like snapshots from a vacation that had never taken place—of strange and exotic buildings, women, food, music, sounds, and smells—all glossed over in that impossibly romantic veneer that only the mind of the untraveled can conjure.

Perhaps he would pawn the hat for pocket money. It appeared to be in good shape, almost new, save for a few scuff marks. Somerset Windgap had not worked in two years. He had once published a dirty novel set in eighteenth-century England called *Sir Cuthbert's Prowls Amongst the Peasantry*, which had paid him a small royalty, but was summarily dismissed by the press. The *New York Times Adult Book Review* particularly objected to his description of the drawing room in which Sir Cuthbert violated the servant, Maggie, as possessing "A Klismos chair of richest rosewood", Klismos chairs not being in popular use until the early 1800s. Hurt and a little indignant, Windgap wrote a letter to the magazine, saying he hardly thought interior design important to the overall thrust of the story, to which the editorial board replied that it "darn well knew what turned a woman on better than Somerset Q. Windgap, thank you very much."

There arose a problem, presently, in that every time Windgap attempted to pick up the hat, it appeared to vanish, only to show up once again in an entirely different spot. At first he thought the wind was to blame, but he had never known wind to be so cunning.

The quicker he worked, the more elusive the hat became, making him change directions again and again, until he no longer knew whether he was coming or going. All at once there was another sharp gust, and the hat was carried up in the air and thrown over the fence of a nearby park. Windgap thought he had seen where the hat had gone, but almost immediately doubt set in, until he began to wonder whether there had ever really been a hat there at all. Dazed and frightened, he raced across the street toward the park's entrance.

It wasn't until he was halfway across the pavement that he caught sight of the bus coming toward him. It appeared as if out of thin air, as if his mind had conjured up the image and somehow made it manifest, so that there was no time to move out of the way. Windgap wasn't sure if he was struck. There was no pain and no injuries appeared anywhere on his body. He looked about himself for some time, but could get no bearing on his surroundings, and began to doubt whether he or the park had ever really existed at all. Nearby was a hat, but it was of a different color and the brim was somewhat wider than he remembered.

Warren Elk heard screams coming from the direction of Glenwood Avenue. Not long after that came the sirens, and the flashing red of an ambulance went racing past, peeking out over the top of the fence surrounding Garfield Park. He watched the lights until they disappeared behind a line of maple trees and allowed himself a few seconds to wonder what had happened, whether anyone had been hurt or killed. Then he pushed the incident out of his mind and focused again on the board in front of him.

His situation appeared hopeless. Elk surveyed his pieces' positions and made a quick evaluation. His king had drifted too far toward the corner and was in danger of being pinned by his opponent's queen and bishop. A knight provided an ineffectual defense, while a single pawn—stranded out on F6—waited to be slaughtered.

"That's it," said Elk. "I've lost."

The old man looked across at him. "You resign?"

"Why not? It's hopeless, isn't it?"

He nodded. "It would appear so. Still, I always like to play my games out to the end. You can never tell what might happen."

"Like what?" said Elk, and chuckled. "You might keel over from a heart attack before you can put me in check?"

"Maybe. Maybe there's a breeze, or a vendor yells something and distracts me. Maybe I give you an opening."

"That's a lot of 'maybes'."

"At worst you might learn something. I've just never seen the percentage in quitting." The old man rose, put on his top hat and adjusted his collar. "Nevertheless, I accept your defeat. Have a good day, sir. I hope we might play again some day."

Elk reached across the table and shook the man's hand. After a few minutes, he took his king and laid the piece on its side. Soon thereafter, a gust of wind blew through the park; the table shook, causing the king to roll—back and forth, back and forth—until at last it toppled over the edge onto the ground. Elk did not bother to retrieve it. He turned around on the bench to face eastward, away from the skyline and the terrible glow of the city.

Across the park, a butterfly skirted the edge of a pond, dipping down towards the water's blue surface, only to pull away sharply at the last second. Warren Elk pulled his coat tight around him as the wind continued to blow, not knowing whether to seek shelter or to leave this place and try his luck on the streets. Everywhere he looked, every moment that he waited seemed fraught with peril. With a despair to fill a thousand hearts, he felt the first few drops of rain beginning to fall.

His Majesty's Royal Mechanic

It all started with a high-pitched whine followed by a low rumbling coming from the undercarriage. I innocently observed that this was often a symptom of worn brake pads, and from that moment on I was the personal mechanic to Magnificent Tumbo, Supreme Leader of the New Democratic Republic of Independent Freedom (NDRIF), or—as President Tumbo fondly referred to it—"home."

Like much of the third world, the NDRIF had few cars, and those it did possess hailed from a bygone and decidedly Soviet era. President Tumbo, being the richest and most powerful man in the country, was owner of the only western automobile inside its borders, a 1986 AMC Eagle. The car had been a gift from the people of the nation to their glorious Leader, the purchase undertaken on their behalf by the Leader's Secretary of the Treasury and paid for by "borrowing" funds from the fledgling State's coffers, the debt for which—by a typically magnanimous decree from Tumbo—had been immediately forgiven.

137

Perhaps it was the prestige of having an American perform such menial tasks, but it wasn't long before the maintenance of the Great Leader's Eagle became the top priority of the NDRIF's government. This was not the way things were supposed to be. My original assignment had been as a development consultant and Chief Advisor to the Vice Chancellor of the Exchequer. But—as my preservice training with Harmony Brigade had taught me—one had to be flexible.

I had stumbled across the Harmony Brigade's website one afternoon while in a fit of depression, having received a stinging rejection letter from the Peace Corps. Despite the assurances and appearance of several of my old college friends, who were now spending their days swilling exotic liquors and cultivating beards all across the globe in the fight against poverty, the Peace Corps *did* have standards. First and foremost among them was a college degree, which—despite more than a year of valiant struggle—I had not been able to obtain. It was humbling to discover that I could not even *give* my time away, and so I spent my subsequent afternoons lounging on the couch with my high school diploma, my thirty-three state university credits, and decidedly few options.

Shrouded in self-pity, I cut myself off from the world, eschewing visitors, the telephone and even e-mail, where constant promises of longer-lasting erections and quick weight-loss solutions only served to underscore my many, God-given shortcomings. It was a week before I could summon the fortitude to check my inbox, but when I finally did I was surprised to find it stuffed full of messages from a mysterious sender named 'Harmony Brigade'. "Peace Corps turned you down?" it said on the subject line, "Click here!" My depression making me more vulnerable to suggestion than usual, I readily complied and was stunned to find the answer to all my questions staring me in the face:

Peace Corps is a world-renowned organization that has been helping people in developing countries for over forty-five years. You probably think you know everything there is to know about this hallowed institution. But did you know that there are countries the Peace Corps deems "too dangerous" to send volunteers, encompassing a population of some half-million people? Where the Peace Corps sees danger, we here at the Harmony Brigade see opportunity.

Harmony Brigade is an organization that sends volunteers to war-torn countries to teach people basic skills, like gardening, crochet, and playground restoration, to help bolster their quality of life. Teach a displaced Amazonian tribesman how to apply for microcredit financing. Help Serbian villagers rid their recently shelled community of unsightly graffiti. The opportunities are limited only by your imagination.

And unlike the Peace Corps, we aren't hung up on fancy 'degrees' and 'qualifications'. Does it take a college degree to pick up a shovel? Harmony Brigade doesn't think so. And neither do the residents of Sudan, Myanmar, Libya, and the various other countries whom we've helped hammer, paint and shovel their way out of despair.

If you think you're up for the challenge, visit our website and apply today. Harmony Brigade—exporting hope to the hopeless since 2005.

Needless to say, I was sold. A ray of hope cut through the gloom as I went to the website and filled out my application, which consisted of my name, address, and phone number. I clicked the submit button, took a quick shower, got dressed, and went out of my apartment for the first time in a week to grab some lunch. When

I returned, I saw the light on my answering machine blinking. It was a message from the Harmony Brigade, telling me I'd been accepted.

The next few days were a blur. I was bussed at my own expense to Harmony Brigade's main office in East New York, where I met with members of the senior administration and received my orientation packet. There, I first learned of my assignment to the New Democratic Republic of Independent Freedom—a country so new it was not yet recognized as a sovereign nation by any other government in the world. I was to be the Harmony Brigade's flagship volunteer in the NDRIF. The fate of the program, and of a quasi-nation, rested on my shoulders.

There was a flight from New York to Dakar, then a bumpy twelve-hour bus ride over sun-baked dirt roads, and before I knew it, I found myself standing in front of a large, oak desk, behind which sat my new boss, Magnificent Tumbo. As I had not slept or shaved in three days, it was with some small measure of disgust that President Tumbo regarded his first real, flesh-and-blood American. "I expected something different," he said, after several minutes' silent contemplation. Pressing a button on the intercom on his desk, he called in his secretary, who was ordered to show me to my quarters and prep me for my work in the Financial Ministry.

Having no background in economics, I was wary about my ability to help in any meaningful way with the finances of the State. But as it turned out, it was only a matter of minutes after meeting my new co-worker—Vice Chancellor of the Exchequer, Mbizi Mwanza—and skimming through the Treasury's books that I observed a critical issue I felt must be addressed.

"You have no money," I pointed out.

"This is not a problem," said Mwanza.

I could see I still had much to learn. For starters, Mwanza informed me that inflation had been outlawed years ago, and we were therefore free to print money to assuage any crisis. With cost no longer an issue, we held a weeklong brainstorming session with the Department of the Interior and gave our stamp of approval to several new projects designed to bolster the nation's infrastructure, including the construction of a fifty-foot, solid-gold statue of the Supreme Leader at the NDRIF's only legal border crossing, that visitors to the country might feel welcome.

It was on our way to the unveiling of the statue that we first noticed the brake trouble that led to my appointment as the Ruler's personal mechanic. But greater car trouble loomed. On a tour of the countryside—a charitable tradition undertaken monthly that rural villagers not be deprived too long of the sight of their Dear Leader—our automobile struck a rock. As we continued down the road the car began to tremble violently, and the acrid smell of scorched rubber wafted past our noses. At last, the Leader ordered the driver to pull over and turn off the engine.

"Mechanic!" he bellowed.

I got out of the car and leaned over to inspect the damage. Just as I had feared, the front, passenger-side tire was shredded to ribbons. When I relayed the information to President Tumbo, he was beside himself with rage.

"Mechanic!" he said. "Remedy this problem!"

"I can't," I said.

"Can't?"

"The tire's completely gone. Without a spare, there's nothing I can do."

"*Tires*," he seethed, his fists clenched. He turned to the Secretary of Transportation, who was riding on the hump. "Arrange transport to the nearest village!" he roared. "This situation will be dealt with immediately."

At the time it seemed to me like a fairly simple situation to deal with, until I learned that the only four American tires the nation possessed were already affixed to the Leader's Eagle. Therefore, by popping, the offending tire had succeeded in crippling the entire automobile fleet of the NDRIF. We proceeded on horseback to the tiny town of Gorel Banu where we spent the night in the home of the mayor, who had been kind enough to remove his family to a dried-out riverbed that we might sleep in relative comfort.

Still furious, President Tumbo called a typically melodramatic press conference the next morning in the village square. "I, Magnificent Tumbo," he said, "being President of your revered Motherland, am the embodiment of the soul and conscience of its esteemed people. As you are—and this I have told you, many times—the chosen race of our Lord God, most Holy of Holies, then I, by extension, am His divine presence here on Earth. Therefore, any insult or slander to my person is tantamount to blasphemy and subject to His divine punishment. I hereby sentence this Michelin model LTX to undergo the ancient ceremony of exorcism, that its soul shall be banished to the fiery pits, tormented until the ends of Time by Satan, the great Deceiver!"

Despite being reared on the State's woefully inaccurate education system, the people of the NDRIF were still well aware that a tire was an inanimate rubber object, and therefore did not possess a soul. Still, they were equally aware that refusal to comply with this order would mean their deaths, and so on the following afternoon the tire was transported back to the capitol building and the ceremony held on the lawn of the Grand Plaza, complete with witch doctor, Catholic priest, and the sacrifice of a virgin nanny goat, while all the while the people wondered if their leader wasn't the dumbest citizen of them all.

Since then my time has been occupied with trying to secure a visa for President Tumbo to visit America, in order to purchase a new set of Michelin all-terrains better suited to the NDRIF's highway system. The Treasury Department has printed an additional two billion banknotes to finance the trip and the paperwork is all taken care of, but issues with U.S. Customs have put the trip on hold for the moment. Turns out none of the representatives we've talked to know how to issue a visa to a citizen of a country that doesn't exist. Just one more reason why my presence here is needed. Though the Peace Corps and the American government might turn a blind eye to the NDRIF, to me it will always be thought of as "home".

Fort Mapleview, the Musical

As the clock tower struck midnight, clanging its pronouncement of a new day over the sleeping heads of the denizens of Fort Mapleview, Fenwick Fingle slipped stealthily through the back door of Mendelssohn's Pub and made his way towards the hotel. When the twelfth and final ring had faded from his ears, an eerie silence descended over the town, amplifying his footsteps and making him cringe at every crackle of dirt or swish of grass that emanated from beneath the soles of his too-small oxfords. His choice of footwear this evening had been too hasty; his feet, constricted and bound like a geisha's, throbbed with every footfall, and the leather soles proved too slippery on the grass and too loud clacking over the pavement. He thought, briefly, about taking them off and padding home in his socks, but the thought of accidentally stepping on a nail or piece of glass and contracting some horrible disease worried him even more than being detected. Not that there was any law against being out after midnight, but in a community as prone to gossip as

Fort Mapleview, public opinion was often the more formidable court in which to be tried.

Besides, there was always the possibility the truth behind his late-night sojourns might come to light, and that was a chance he simply could not take. For Fenwick Fingle was not out engaging in boozy revelries or making the acquaintance of some painted vixen of dubious pedigree. His transgression was something far more pedestrian, and yet, universally reviled, the mere mention of which was enough to imbue speaker and listener alike with red-faced shame. In a shadowy, back booth of this colonial watering hole, he met three times a week with his partner—a gaunt, balding intellectual named Archibald Sump—to put the finishing touches on a project six long months in the making.

Fenwick Fingle was writing a script.

Hardly something to be embarrassed about, you might think to yourself, but one must always keep in mind the regard in which hardworking, provincial townsfolk hold flights of artistic fancy. For centuries before Augustus, the Romans had regarded writing as a vaguely decadent and contemptible pursuit—something better left to the effeminate Greeks—and there were many in Fort Mapleview who shared this view today. To a man spending ten hours a day running a powdered metal press, "dramatist" hardly registers as a profession at all, let alone a legitimate one. But what really made Fingle's endeavor a potential powder keg waiting to explode was his choice of subject— the history of Fort Mapleview itself. It was a subject on which the citizens of the town had formed a clear consensus and that was dear to their hearts. No one, least of all an outsider like Fingle, was permitted to take liberties.

The town of Fort Mapleview had, as its name suggests, been founded by the British Royal Army as a military fortification during the early years of the French and Indian War. Its name derived from the lone maple tree, that—according to Lieutenant Colonel Benjamin P. Brathwaite's harrowing account of frontier life—was "all that God had deemed permissible to distract us from the endless expanse of grassy hill and dale that was our constant companion lo those many years". Since those days, that singular maple had multiplied and spread into a dense forest, surrounding the outskirts of the town like a barricading army. In fact, it was a common joke amongst Fort Mapleviewees (as citizens, for lack of a better term, called themselves), when entertaining a visiting history buff, to say that "you can't see Brathwaite's maple for the trees". At least it would have been common, had more than a handful of tourists bothered to visit Fort Mapleview in any given year. Having been miles from the scene of any significant fighting, life in Fort Mapleview in the mid-eighteenth century had consisted chiefly of whittling and learning to enjoy eating corn.

Few firsthand accounts of those early days survived down through the years, the major exception being Brathwaite's exhaustive diary, which by now was regarded as gospel by the town elders. For all of its 928 pages, it was decidedly short on dramatic action, as this fairly representative passage demonstrates:

Sept. 13, 1754 – Cloudy; slight drizzle in the afternoon. Was summoned to the North Bastion by Private Jameson just after breakfast. Upon alighting, observed a squirrel making its way across the grass toward the foot of the wall. Was questioned by Jameson as to protocol, but could ascertain nothing from officer's manual regarding rodent-based incursions. Prepared memo to be sent to General Braddock requesting orders. Returned to North Bastion to receive update on situation, but was told the squirrel had pulled back and was retreating in a southwesterly direction.

A scant clay for Fingle to mold. Renowned though he was in off-Broadway circles and in his post as chair of NYU's drama department, he was, like any writer, a slave to his source material. When he had been approached in the summer by the Ohio Valley Council of the Arts to do a production celebrating Fort Mapleview's 250th anniversary, he had jumped at the chance, enamored as he was with historical dramas. Naturally, he had assumed the project had the blessing of the mayor and the towns-people, but on his arrival in Fort Mapleview it soon became clear that his presence had not been expected, nor was it particularly desired. Like any small-town folk, their solid upbringing compelled them to show a certain level of hospitality to this interloper with the fancy dress and mannered speech. But it was a decidedly thin-lipped hospitality, more godly duty than brotherly love, and every polite inquiry about his well-being seemed to possess at the end the unspoken question, *"And when will you be leaving?"*

His meeting with the town council had not gone as planned. In great detail, he had outlined his plans to turn Fort Mapleview's founding into a stage musical, considering the presentation to be little more than a formality. Imagine his shock, then, when his request to peruse the historical society's archives and town records was declined. Fingle was more than welcome to stay on for a while, take in the sights and experience Fort Mapleview's legendary hospitality, but he would receive no official assistance from local officials. What's more, the council had serious doubts that any private citizens would be interested in talking to him either.

There was little trust in these parts, they continued, for big city types from the East Coast treating their lives as fodder for a story. Faced with this, there was little Fingle could do but thank the council for its time and retire to the room he had rented at the Lamplight Bed & Breakfast.

With a week's lodging paid and his plans in shambles, Fingle decided there was nothing for it but to take the council's advice. He spent the next two days perusing the Mapleview Botanical Gardens and the various shops along Main Street, and enjoying a late-night *digestif* at Mendelssohn's, seemingly the only place in Fort Mapleview where one could purchase alcohol. It was sometime during lunch on the third day, munching a soggy approximation of a corned beef sandwich, that Fingle realized he was bored stiff and resolved to catch the next plane back to New York. Fortuitous, then, that Archibald Sump picked that very moment to enter the Lamplight and sit down at Fingle's table.

He spoke hurriedly, but firmly, leaving Fingle little room for questions—Sump was a professor of anthropology at nearby Clearwater Community College. He was also one of the few people with access to the town's historical records.

"I grew up here," said Sump. "They trust me." He spoke with a glass of water to his lips, concealing his mouth. "I've taken an interest in this project of yours."

"You want to help me?" said Fingle.

Sump nodded. "I spent some time on the East Coast myself, you know. My BA is from Princeton, class of '74. I've always had a soft spot for stage musicals."

"Can you get me in to see the archives?"

"Even better—I'll bring the archives to you." Sump's eyes scanned the room. "Not here, though. You're being watched by the staff. I'm taking a chance just meeting you like this. Do you know Mendelssohn's? Good. Meet me there tonight at ten o'clock in the back room. We should be safe there. Fort Mapleview's a conservative town. No one who's in good with the mayor or the council would be out at a drinking establishment at such a late hour. See you then."

That night they met for the first time. Sump had brought with him, concealed beneath his coat, the first installment of Colonel Brathwaite's diary, covering his initial deployment up to the "Great Acorn Shortage of 1753". Fingle scanned the documents, scribbling down notes, with Sump clarifying the more obscure references.

They went on meeting this way, the days stretching into weeks, then months. Fingle continued to extend his stay at the Lamplight, dispelling any suspicion as to his motives by touting the beneficial effects of the air and greenery upon his health. This, the townsfolk accepted without question, imagining New York to be enshrouded in a perpetual veil of filth and moral depravity.

And then, suddenly, one day he was gone. There had been no goodbyes, no words of parting. Not even the owner of the Lamplight had seen him leave; his bill had been paid in advance, and she had entered his room that morning to find his bed made and his belongings gone, without so much as a note of explanation. It was as if he had vanished into thin air, and though it made for some heady gossip around the lunch counter of the Do or Diner for quite some time, eventually people forgot all about Fenwick Fingle and his project and got back to the daily business of living.

When, exactly, the tourists first started showing up was difficult to pinpoint. What started as a trickle of bemused outsiders in tacky shorts and cheap sunglasses soon became a torrent; busloads of people from all corners of the country, cameras and guidebooks in hand, flooded over the town, a loud-talking, gum-chewing tsunami from which the local populace could find no refuge. They made strange requests, asking to see the inn where George Washington got drunk and scribbled on a cocktail napkin the first draft of what would become the Declaration of Independence, or the glade where Colonel Brathwaite secretly married the Chippewa princess, Methoataske, against the wishes of their disapproving peers. The fact that no such things ever took place, but were the invention of Fenwick Fingle, whose *Fort Mapleview, the Musical*, was breaking all manner of box-office records, hardly dampened the enthusiasm of the visitors, whose zeal and disposable cash soon led to a cottage industry selling trinkets and guided tours of wholly imaginary events. A string of luxury hotels sprang up, putting the struggling Lamplight out of business, and ground broke on the 'Princess Methoataske Casino and Resort', with Wayne Newton booked to perform opening night. As time passed and the money flowed in, a statue of Fingle—the patron saint of Fort Mapleview—was erected in the town square. It was, as the town archives would record it, the beginning of a new Golden Age.

Decline and Fall

I

Edwin Block had taken a house overlooking the sea.

This change in setting had been at the behest of his editor, the incomparable Mr. Sams, with the purpose of helping him complete his latest literary endeavor, a novelization of Gibbon's *The Decline and Fall of the Roman Empire*, and had been selected for its location not five miles north of Hadrian's Wall. It was the editor's sincere belief that being in such close proximity to this relic from the Age of the Antonines could not help but inspire his charge to channel the poet Ovid, who had been quite a sensation in his day, or so Mr. Sams had heard. A tall task, some would argue, for a writer whose previous high-water mark was the tea-cosy thriller *The Butler Knocks But Thrice*, which one prominent critic described as "something far less than Christie". ("Still, there it is," said Block at the time, "me and Agatha Christie.") It should be noted that through this belief, Mr. Sams exposed a naivety incongruous with his reputation, for the fact of the matter was that Edward Block cared little for history, less for Rome, and not a cat's bollocks for Hadrian or his blasted pile of stones. What made Edwin Block tick was money, and nothing got the public dipping into their wallets like a good sword-and-sandal epic, especially one with *D & F*'s superior brand recognition. "This one's in the bag," he thought to himself, as he signed the papers for his million-dollar advance.

The project had certainly received enough attention in the press. There were some, mostly academicians and bookish types, who took a dim view of the proceedings. Block wasn't surprised. Their verbal slings and arrows proved rubber-tipped, for Edwin Block understood better than anyone the maxim that there's no such thing as bad publicity. Still, he had to admit he was hard-pressed to find the advantages in a prominent Oxford professor referring to him as "Edwin Schlock" in an *Atlantic Monthly* piece about the "contemporary blockbuster".

But wherever money and attention concentrate there are sure to be admirers as well as critics. After a profile of the writer had appeared in *Vanity Fair* (with, amongst other things, a full-page photograph of Block in a wind-tunnel, his shirt inexplicably unbuttoned to his navel, bearing the caption "Intellectually Stimulating") he was paid a personal visit at his Long Island residence by an obscure Danish countess, who professed to be "much interested in writings, and all manner of these things." Though certainly older than Block by a few years, she possessed a vaguely royal attractiveness; Block was reminded of a more fragile Jacqueline Onassis, and spent much of the afternoon sifting through her ungrammatical English and trying to turn the conversation to matters sexual. Unsuccessful, he nevertheless earned a devoted fan, and promised to personally mail Ms. Rasmussen an autographed copy of the novel as soon as he received the first batch from the printer.

Of course, before any book could be sent, it first had to be written. This was the part of being a writer Block liked least. There was something about the blank page—with its infinite possibilities for giving form to his inner, creative voice—that made him desire a stiff scotch and water. This he now poured for himself, consuming the drink in what some people might describe a "desperate" gulp, before settling down to work. Luckily, he was not adrift without oars. Mr. Sams had faxed him a list a of directives drawn up by his publisher's marketing department in New York to aid him in his quest. Directive number one: 'Lose the declining and falling'.

"Won't that prove rather difficult?" asked Block, who had phoned Mr. Sams in confusion. "I mean, we'll need another title, won't we?"

"Keep the title," said Sams. "Marketing says that's very important. Anyone calls you on it, just say you were being ironic. That's a direct quote, Eddie: 'I was being ironic'."

Block frowned into the receiver. "This sounds like it's going to require revisions."

"What revisions? A war comes along, Rome kicks some ass. Easy!"

"What's this about here?" Block ran his finger along the print. "Directive number three: 'Push Caesar's love life'."

"I know, I know . . ." said Sams. "I told them you're not a sex writer, but they insisted. It seems a couple of studios are already jockeying to get the rights to this thing, but they want a part where they can cast a strong, female lead. Don't worry about turning anyone on. Just get Caesar in the bedroom once in a while and let him do his thing."

"But Julius Caesar's dead before any of this takes place."

"What do you mean he's 'dead'?"

"I mean he's not alive."

"What about Cleopatra and Mark Anthony and that bunch?"

"Antony," said Block.

"What?"

"Mark *Antony*."

"What's that, a Jersey accent?"

"That's his name," said Block. "It's right here in the footnotes."

"Aw, crap! Look, I'll call you back..."

There was a click, and the line went dead. Block put down the receiver and went back to his desk. The screen was just as blank as he had left it. "Screens," thought Block.

Procrastination is surely an underrated form of genius, for when a man desires not to do something, his ability to invent distractions, excuses and self-deceptions surpasses the most fertile minds of literature's canon. So it was that Edwin Block developed the theory that a stroll through the country, perhaps even down to the seaside to imbibe its salty air, would do his constitution a world of good. And since he was already out (or *would* already be out; Block was nothing if not forward-thinking), it certainly wouldn't hurt to visit the nearby village—an enchanting little hamlet with a name like 'South Wussex', or something— and introduce himself to some of the locals. If this was to be his home for the next year, he had no intention of spending that time in isolation. Having adapted *Bleak House* as a romantic comedy for Warner Brothers only a few years back, Block was not unacquainted with the character of the rural English village; he knew that most people would already be out at the pubs this time of night, those quaint, one-room watering holes with their hearths roaring in the corner, their peasants singing 'Lish Young Buy-A-Broom' to the ghosts of their uncles, and those curious names that were little more than a combination of two unrelated animals, like 'The Fox & Hedgehog'. Though experience had shown that with Edwin Block, one drink led to two, and two drinks to twenty, he was not in the least bit worried that this eventuality might interfere with the writing process. Quite the contrary, science had proven (and Block was nothing if not a believer in science) that alcohol actually *lowered* inhibitions, and inhibitions were one thing Block needed decidedly less of at the moment. No, pubs were quite good for one's writing. Shakespeare wrote in pubs.

So it was that later that evening, with the countryside trod and the sea air sniffed, Edwin Block made a beeline for the nearest drinking house. This he located mere seconds after arriving on the outskirts of town, if a town the size of South Wussex, or whatever it was called, could indeed be said to possess "outskirts". It was a painfully cubic structure of red brick that had shunned the time-worn inspiration of the animal kingdom and derived its moniker instead from two seemingly random, inanimate objects, namely The Harpoon and Barrel. Upon further reflection, Block was able to identify a vaguely nautical theme underlying the choice, a theory which was proved correct as he entered the establishment to find a bevy of nets, rods, reels, and framed photographs of deep-sea trawlers adorning the walls, not to mention the sizeable stuffed swordfish which dangled from the ceiling rafters, mouth agape. On first spying the beast, Block felt a flutter pass through his stomach; its eyes seemed to be looking directly into Block's, its terrified expression warning him to turn back now and walk out the door, before it was too late. But while Edwin Block knew little of superstition and even less of the sea, he felt the omens of a swordfish could be safely dismissed as specious.

Block took a seat at a corner table that afforded him a commanding view of the room. One could have debated the benefits of such a position. Of the twenty or so tables that filled The Harpoon and Barrel only three were populated, and these by a singular type of man, whose scruffy beard, weathered face and knee-length slicker made him seem more like a prop—placed there specifically to add to the general ambience of the place— than a real customer. "Bluff old salts" is how Block would have described them had they been characters in one of his novels.

A waiter came around to take Block's order. Acknowledging the universal distaste for tourists, Block did his best to go local.

"I should fancy an ale," he said.

"What sort of ale should you fancy?" asked the waiter, coming as close as anyone ever has to verbally rolling their eyes.

Block ignored this and affected deep consideration. "I think a pint of your *finest* ale should do nicely."

"A pint of our finest ale," said the waiter. "Certainly, sir. May I compliment the gentleman's taste."

Block allowed him to do so, and marveled that a young man so recently removed from his teenage years could be possessed of so much jaded contempt.

Faced with these inauspicious surroundings, it was fortunate for Block he had not come empty-handed. Indeed, tucked away in a pocket of his overcoat was the second volume of Gibbon's classic history. Block was embarrassed to admit that in the six months since the novelization was first proposed he had progressed no further in his reading of the original *Decline and Fall* than the midpoint of chapter seven. But it wasn't that the exploits of Maximin and Balbinus had bogged down a mind unequal to their comprehension (as his critics would no doubt suggest if they ever learned of his ignorance). No, Edwin Block's crisis was not intellectual, but moral. Exactly when it happened Block could not say, but he suspected it had started as early as the first sentence; pouring through Gibbon's learned treatise, marveling at the style and wit with which that giant of the Enlightenment brought to life fourteen hundred years of human history, not to mention the painstaking research that had been required to render it accurate (the footnotes alone made Block tremble), had caused a subtle but profound shift to take place in the way he viewed his life's work. Quite simply, Edwin Block was ashamed. For the majority of his life he had viewed the enterprise of writing solely by its potential to make him money. Any notions of beauty or artistic merit were quickly dismissed; indeed, it was only when Edwin Block discovered the secret that it was the truly *mediocre* writers who ascended to fame and fortune in their own lifetime that he seized upon it as his chosen profession, and guarded his profound revelation by adopting the air of a pompous, pseudo-intellectual. Rather than bringing about his ruin, it was absolutely crucial to his success that Block allow the sycophantic praise of his fans to warp his self-perception, for only by maintaining the illusion that he possessed some unique talent or gift could he keep the public from realizing he was nothing but a glorified huckster, with little more to recommend him than his ability to lift a pencil.

And it may not come as a surprise, based on such evidence, that Edwin Block had never been much of a reader. Perhaps that was why his introduction to Gibbon had rattled him so deeply and totally. Faced with the product of a lifetime's passionate labor, how could he bear the thought that on his deathbed he would have little to look back upon for solace than tawdry, supermarket filler like *Unclasp Thy Bodice*?

His ever-slowing pace, then, was not a matter of indifference, but of survival. Every newly read chapter of *Decline and Fall* was a fresh crack in his once unshakable self-confidence; his will to continue, the very future of the novelization, hung in the balance, and Edwin Block simply could not afford at this point to develop a conscience and walk away. For in the rarified world of the rich and famous, even the most celebrated author earns a comparative pittance, and Block's lifestyle—filled as it was with perversions and creature comforts that would have made a sultan blush at his immodesty—kept him trapped in a perpetual, financial purgatory.

There were alternatives to hawking mass-market bilge —turningover a new leaf, for example. But looking around at the sad and bleary faces in The Harpoon and Barrel, Edwin Block knew he could never condescend to join their ranks. After all, the rich and poor partake of the same vices, but it is only those with money whom society forgives. Block did not bother waiting for his drink, which the obstinate young waiter still had yet to bring to his table. He no longer required its bracing effect. A decision had been reached, and while it may have done little to soothe the pangs of remorse he felt, it was nevertheless final and irrevocable. Never do anything halfway, his father had once told him. For better or worse the die had been cast, and Edwin Block was prepared to meet his fate with stoic resignation.

He returned home well after sundown. As if awaiting his arrival, the phone began to ring the second he came through the door. Block went into the kitchen and picked up the receiver. It was Sams again, calling from New York.

"So," said Block, "have you sorted out our Caesar problem?"

"I've got one word for you," said Sams. "Flashbacks!"

Flashbacks indeed. Edwin Block hung up the phone, went immediately to his desk, and began to type.

II

Mr. Sams hung up the phone and immediately began emptying the contents of a bottle of James A. Prospector's Olde-Timey Bourbon into a waiting brandy snifter. His wife, Marlene, watched from the couch with mild interest, or at least with less disinterest than she felt for the poorly written, first-person account of "One Woman's Struggle With Ibuprofen" she had been skimming in the latest issue of *Cosmo*. A connoisseur of vices, yet adherent to none, it was not uncommon to see Sams taking a sip of the hard stuff before three in the afternoon, but only news of a very singular kind could lead him to seek the company of a libation as monumental as the one he now prepared. Marlene searched his face for a clue as to whether this blackout-to-be was of a celebratory or conciliatory nature; usually some hint lay in the eyebrows, but this time they proved less than prophetic.

"Something the matter?" she asked him at last.

Sams turned and exposed his teeth. "You hear me call you a whore yet?"

"Oh," she said, with a faint smile, "then it's good news."

"The *best*." Sams took his drink and walked across the room to where a framed copy of Gadstone's *Bricking Up the Caledonians* hung above the mantle. He had purchased it from an auction at Sotheby's not long after the *Decline and Fall* project had been green-lighted. Marlene could not understand the compulsion that led to these lavish expenditures; other than money, Sams expressed no passionate interest in any subject. His life was little more than a collage, built from the fragments of the works he had represented over the years, a sort of Renaissance man by proxy. The breadth of his knowledge and eclectic nature of his possessions, rather than marking him as a man of voracious mental appetites, betrayed a shallow, parasitic personality. Sams was a master of the random fact; judiciously inserted into the middle of a conversation, dispensed at cocktail parties like hors d'oveurs, he cultivated what was surely his one true talent, that of appearing to know absolutely everything. But rarely was deeper understanding pursued with anything approaching the zeal he reserved for a stiff whisky sour.

"I told you that wall would squeeze it out of him!" said Sams. He studied the painting for a moment, raised his glass to the triumphant emperor and expelled a brittle laugh. "Hadrian, I could kiss your ugly mug!"

"Edwin's coming along then?" asked Marlene.

"Coming along? He's finished the thing! We'll be going to print by June!"

"Finished?" Marlene straightened herself on the couch. "It's only been three months."

"I know! Can you believe it?"

"He novelized *The Decline and Fall of the Roman Empire* in three months?"

This question Marlene accompanied with a severe squint, which she then aimed down at the floor, as if the answer lay somewhere beneath the linoleum tiling. Sams knew that squint; it meant his wife was thinking. At no time did he find her less attractive than these rare moments of pensiveness. The cognitive process fit her like a ten-dollar suit.

"What?" he asked.

"Well, *The Decline and Fall of the Roman Empire* is a pretty big book..."

"I'm listening."

"And it seems to me that in order to turn such a big book into a novel..."

"Yeah?"

"It would probably take more than three months. To do it well, I mean."

"Ha!" Sams gave a sweeping bow and gestured to the telephone. "Exhibit A for the defense!"

"What," said Marlene, "Edwin? All he said was that he was finished. You don't know if what he wrote is any good."

"Marlene, Edwin Block is a professional. You know how much money he brings in?"

"What's money have to do with art?"

"Oh, here we go!" Sams began to pace in front of the couch, with the cocksure strut of a man who has recently consumed a mild quantity of very cheap bourbon. "Another high-minded critic, right here under my roof! Why don't you take some art to the supermarket this weekend, see how many groceries it buys you? It was Edwin's money that paid for those new shoes you're wearing, you know."

"These shoes cost twenty-nine dollars."

"That's right, *dollars*. Not sonnets, not watercolors." Sams took the deep breath which precedes soliloquy. "I know how you feel about me. You think I'm hard-hearted, callous, blind to beauty, obsessed with material things. Maybe you're right, maybe I am. But it's only because of people like me that people like you can exist. It's because of my industriousness that you have leisure to sit around admiring "the speckled thrush's song", or whatever you were going on about last week. What? All right, speckled *warbler*, who gives a shit? You want to know the truth? I couldn't care less if Block's novel is any good. I couldn't care less if he copied the New York phone directory verbatim. The fact is, this book is going to sell. It's going to make us rich, Marlene. I may not know much, but I know that.."

"We're already rich," she muttered.

"Then it'll make us even richer!" he snapped. "I know that pains you. I know it pains you to even hear the word 'money'. Perhaps I should start spelling it, the way you do around a little kid: M-O-N-E-Y."

"My dear husband, you've been practicing!"

"Oh, ha ha!" said Sams. "Very much 'ha'! I had no idea twenty-six years ago that I was marrying Oscar Wilde! A pity you inherited the wit without the femininity!"

Having landed that rather pointed low blow, Sams started quickly from the room. When he was halfway through the door he stopped. "Oh, and by the way, 'novelize' isn't even a word!"

"What?"

"'Novelize'."

"Are you sure?"

"I don't think so."

"I thought it meant to drastically change something. Like how those miracle knives on TV novelize the way you chop vegetables."

"No, they *revolutionize* the way you chop vegetables."

"Oh, you're right. Well I *know* I've heard it somewhere before. Do you remember where I put the Scrabble dictionary?"

Sams rolled his eyes and slammed the door on his way out.

When Mr. Sams needed to unwind, he took a walk through Burberry Park. It was neither the largest park in the city nor the nearest to where he lived, nor was it—by any conventional standards—the most beautiful. But there was something about the position of the trees, the way their branches filtered the light and shrouded the footpath below in otherworldly gloom, and the almost constant breeze that added an unnatural chill to the air, that made one think of autumn. Sams rather enjoyed the quiet solemnity of that season, not so bombastic as summer's swimming pools and screaming children, nor so cruel as winter's paralyzing cold, nor so trite as spring's flowery dalliances. Burberry Park lent itself to quiet reflection, and despite his wife's characterization of him as a superficial money-grubber, Sams found no greater solace than treading its softly undulating hills, alone but for his thoughts.

It was also where he met his twenty-year old mistress, Suzette.

That Suzette was French should be obvious to even the most casual student of anthropology, and as anyone who traffics in cultural stereotypes knows, the French are well-versed in the ways of love. Though her supple, tawny form was enough to make Gandhi take up firebombing, what Sams appreciated most about Suzette was her complete lack of standards. Despite the fact that in proportion and aspect he was not so different from your average, run-of-the-mill, Atlantic bull walrus, Mr. Sams found little trouble convincing Suzette to do to him things the Marquis de Sade would have found tasteless. All she required in exchange for these services was to know that Sams cared for her, and though he was a busy man and had little time to spend in her company, it was a mark of her character that she never once complained, contenting herself with the occasional platinum necklace, Versace gown, or two-week getaway to the Spanish Riviera he offered as consolation.

Sams checked his watch and hurried down the walkway towards their usual meeting place, by the statue of Faustina near the southeast gate. He was very much alone this afternoon, his footsteps clearly audible above the occasional bird call and soft rustling of leaves. Mounting a footbridge, which joined the opposing banks of a small, manmade pond, he paused to look down at the school of koi darting to and fro in their graceless, unwieldy manner. He was about to continue on, but something held him to the spot; whether it was the placidity of the park or the waning effects of the bourbon, Sams slipped into that semi-lucid state which lends itself to meditative thought. It occurred to him (and perhaps this was not such a novel concept, yet even the most timeworn ideas—for one who has not been previously exposed to them—carry the profound impact of revelation) that a man's life was worth little more than the barely sentient hunks of meat swimming hither and thither beneath him. Were fish meat, he wondered? Catholics certainly didn't think so. If not meat, then what? Rubber? Plastic? Sams chuckled at the absurdity of the idea. He had always disliked Catholics.

But neither biological nor theological semantics altered the fundamental truth he had hit upon: it was only by a man's *deeds* that his life gained meaning. What, then, had been the deeds of Mr. Sams; what exactly was his life worth? He shuddered as he realized he was having an "existential crisis", a term he had picked up from an author many years ago—an author, it should be noted, he had decided not to represent. "Here's an existential crisis for you," Sams had written in his rejection letter. "How can a man afford to buy groceries when he writes third-rate Camus imitations no publisher would touch with a ten-foot pole? I suggest you ponder this one deeply." No doubt that young man, if he could see Sams now, would be savoring his karmic dessert.

Faced with the profound truth of his own insignificance, Sams decided to call it a miss and indulge his sexual appetites. He found Suzette toeing the grass in the usual spot, looking even more sullen and pitiful than he remembered; as he approached her, he was alarmed to find that she was crying.

"Aw crap!" he said. "What now?"

"I am looking at this statue."

"Well knock it off, for Christ's sake!"

"It's too late," she pouted. "I am already quite sad."

Sams sighed. "Okay, I'll bite. *Why* are you sad?"

"This statue..." Suzette ran her hand over Faustina's marble leg. "It is so beautiful."

"Are you kidding me? Look at the honker on that broad!" Sams jerked a thumb at Faustina's honker. "And that hairdo! She looks like Ben Franklin, for crying out loud!"

"Oh kumquat, sometimes you speak such stupidness!"

It was an annoying tendency of Suzette's to call her lovers by the names of exotic fruits and vegetables.

"All right," snorted Sams. "So she's a real dish. Why get all weepy-eyed about it?"

"Look here." She pointed to a bronze plaque mounted below on the pedestal. "This statue was built in 1902. It is more than one hundred years old."

"Ah..."

"One hundred years old, and it has not aged a day. While every minute that passes my skin grows more wrinkled, my muscles more flabby and loose."

"Hey," said Sams, "you're having an existential crisis!"
Suzette nodded gravely.

"I just had one a few minutes ago. Don't sweat it, they pass pretty quickly."

"Not mine. I will never be happy again."

"Aw, come here darling! Let old Sammy Wams cheer you up!"

At this suggestion, Suzette burst into tears. It was not the reaction old Sammy Wams had been hoping for.

"It is not fair!" she sobbed. "Why may she stay young and beautiful while I must grow old?"

"For starters," said Sams, "how about the fact that you're a human being and she's a big *rock*."

"Humph! Are you going to mock me now?"

Never renowned for his verbal thrust-and-parry, Sams was surprised to find several witty retorts on hand to lob at his hapless opponent. It crushed him to waste such a rare opportunity, but try as he might he could feel nothing but sympathy for the poor, pathetic creature in front of him, sniffling liberally into the confines of her embroidered silk handkerchief.

"Naw," he said, sitting down on one of the wooden benches that lined the walk. He reached out and put his hand on her arm. "I know how you feel. Come on, sit down here a minute."

Suzette did as commanded, momentarily stunned out of her sadness by this sudden and unexpected tenderness from Mr. Sams. She perched delicately on the edge of the bench and waited for him to continue.

"Let me ask you something," he said, after a moment's pause. "What do you think of me?"

"How do you mean?" asked Suzette.

"I mean, what's your opinion of me? Do you respect me?"

"Sure, sure I do."

"Yeah?" Sams nodded as he mulled this over. "Why?"

"You are a very successful man."

"You mean money?"

"Not just money." Suzette's face lit up as she shifted her focus away from Time's inexorable march; such is the capriciousness of youth! "You work with books. That's ever-so-important. I just can't think of anything more important. I adore books, but I'm simply not smart enough to be a writer, or an editor like you are."

"What do you think of the idea of writing a novel about ancient Rome based on a famous history book?"

"I think it sounds marvelous!"

"Well, that's what I'm editing right now."

"Oh, pomegranate, what is it called?"

Sams squirmed slightly, speaking the words as if it were a confession. "At the moment, *The Decline and Fall of the Roman Empire – The Novel.*"

"How grand!"

"You think so?"

"Oh yes!" Suzette's eyes widened in that naïve way that both exasperated and charmed Mr. Sams. "Rome sounds so *incredibly* grand, but I don't know a thing about it!"

"Why not read a history book?"

Suzette scrunched up her face.

"But you'd read this novel?"

"Of course! Literature is much more beautiful than history. I only care for beautiful things."

"So by reading this novel, you'd be learning things about Rome you wouldn't have known otherwise?"

"Oh, I hope so! I want to know everything about it! Like her!" Suzette turned her attention back to the statue. "Faustina. She was Roman, wasn't she?"

Sams shrugged.

"*Rome*," she sighed. "Caesar, and the Coliseum, and gladiators, and Helen of Troy, and Shakespeare..."

"Hell of a town."

"We should go there someday!"

"What, Rome?"

"Oh yes!" Suzette brought her legs up and knelt on the bench, clutching Mr. Sams' forearm. "I hear it's ever so lovely this time of year."

"Yeah? Who do you hear that from?"

"A girl hears things."

Sams grunted. "And I suppose *I* would be footing the bill?"

"Oh, papaya, how can you think about money when we're talking of Rome?"

"Rome is money, sweetie! Quite a lot of it. So are you, I might add. What the hell am I going to get out of all this?"

Suzette grinned like a tigress that's cornered a gazelle. As her head sank slowly towards Mr. Sams lap, he weighed the relative merits of the idea that he was an educator. It was a different light than any in which he had ever viewed himself. How many other young men and women like Suzette had read through the works he had edited and learned something new about the world? How many dull happenings of a bygone era had he helped make relevant with the trappings of artistic beauty? Before he could answer there was a blinding white flash, and all existentialism melted in the glorious wellspring of carnal release. Life, decided Sams with his last cognizant thought, still had some meaning after all.

III

It was one of those days that started out badly, continued to be bad well into the afternoon, and by the time evening came around remained decidedly bad. Dawn had brought with it the absence of a familiar and comforting sensation, which—as the sands of sleep fell slowly from Malcolm Bowles's eyes—morphed into the concrete and infinitely more distressing absence of his girlfriend, Patty. In a semi-lucid haze he had groped about her side of the mattress, finding little more than the still-warm indentation where she had been sleeping, a ghostly imprint left there to remind him of her supple (for a gal from Barnsley, at least) figure, which he would never again have the pleasure of touching.

Of course, that distressing development had yet to reveal itself. It was not until Bowles's hand reached the vicinity of Patty's pillow that he encountered, in place of her head, something small and rectangular, rather thin, which made a brittle, "papery" sound as he fingered it. It was a testament to Bowles's pragmatism that not even in the deepest recesses of his heart did he harbor the hope that he had somehow confused his girlfriend with a sheet of paper. As the old saying goes, if it feels like paper, and it sounds like paper, then it's probably a note from Patty telling Malcolm she's leaving him because of his excessive drinking and pathetic obsession with being a writer.

Once again, the maxims of our ancestors proved themselves relevant. Malcolm, sitting bolt upright now, read and reread each line of Patty's admittedly tactful dissection of his faults. And many were the lines. "To achieve greatness, one must be willing to walk through fire"—Bowles could not remember where he had heard this quote, but he now found himself, along with his grand ambition, amidst some truly formidable flames. That Patty had neither called into question the size of— nor the degree of mastery with which he used—his genitalia was about the nearest thing to a silver lining that could be gleaned from her overwhelmingly negative dissertation. Yet such a crude attack would have been welcome compared to the subtle, yet unrelenting denunciation of something he held far more dear—his ability as a writer.

"It's not that I'm saying you aren't a good writer," began one line, which Malcolm understood to say exactly the opposite. "But there are *so many* people out there writing a book, trying to catch a break. And let's face it, people just don't read like they used to. You're twenty-six years old now, and waiting tables in some village bar just isn't going to provide the kind of life a girl like me needs, or a guy like you deserves. This isn't London, you know. Hell, this isn't even Barnsley. There aren't a lot of tips to be had in West Ussex. You can't make a go of it off the few shillings those same four or five old drunks slap on the table at the end of the night, assuming they're still conscious enough to do even that much. I moved out here with you because you asked me to, as an act of faith, to show you that I was willing to sacrifice some of the things I wanted in order to be with you. But there's a thin line between faith and stupidity. Maybe that's something you need to think about. Twenty-three rejections doesn't mean your book isn't good, but it certainly suggests that it's something publishers aren't interested in. I'm still not sure why you can't keep on with writing in another town, or with another job, but I am sure that if your decision is to keep things the way they are then I can't be a part of your life anymore. I hope, for your sake, that I end up being wrong about all of this."

Love, Patty. Malcolm folded up the note and placed it on the nightstand next to the bed. He could honestly say he was neither shocked nor heartbroken by Patty's departure; his reaction consisted only of a dull ache somewhere near the pit of his stomach, resulting in part from his newfound loneliness and the loss of a longtime companion, but principally from the fact that every single thing she had written about him was true. His O-levels were impeccable. His father had connections with the Finance Ministry. There were far bigger and better things he could be doing than slinging ale for a bunch of dodgy old gits with emphysema, poor grammar and wrinkles deeper than the space between a pair of couch cushions. And drinking the ale himself was not one of those things. Without even knowing it he had put on ten pounds since first starting at The Harpoon and Barrel, and while it barely showed on his still-athletic frame, the sluggishness and depression that had accompanied it were much harder to mask. Bowles knew there was nothing revelatory about the idea that depression leads to drinking, which leads to more depression and still more drinking, but to find himself caught within this vicious cycle was a profound and startling reality to face.

But it was never about career aspirations for Malcolm Bowles, about nabbing an entry-level job in some stuffy office and clawing his way up to middle management. It had always been about the writing. Here, too, he was a failure. At least a failure in Patty's eyes, not to mention his mother's, father's, most of his old classmates', and, increasingly, his own. In his more lucid moments he reminded himself that many now-canonical writers had compiled stacks of rejection letters early in their career that would have put his to shame. Voltaire, he remembered reading somewhere, had been told to sod off no less than fifty-seven times before finding an editor willing to publish. The downside to this line of thinking was that it required Bowles to put himself in the same category as Voltaire. There were writers throughout history whose work was so original, so groundbreaking, that publishers were terrified to touch it, and for every one of them, there had also existed at least a million writers whose work was complete and utter pants. All twenty-three rejections meant was that twenty-three different editors felt it was in their best interests not to publish Bowles' novel, and that there now existed twenty-three less chances for him to one day realize his dream. Twenty-three rather sarcastic nails in the coffin.

The twenty-fourth nail arrived later that morning. Malcolm went out to check his mailbox and found a large, manila envelope marked 'Bosrum & Sons Publishing Co.' crammed inside. There was no way, practically, he could possibly know whether a piece of paper bearing the one-word message, "Seriously?", was the most humiliating rejection letter ever received by an aspiring writer, but he was fairly certain Voltaire had at least been shown the consideration of a complete sentence when being turned down.

The only other mail was Bowles's weekly copy of the *West Ussex Bugler*, the town's lone newspaper. In his bleaker periods, when pessimism reigned and the chance of capping a book deal seemed as remote as an afternoon stroll through the Martian countryside, Bowles sometimes considered the possibility of taking a job with *The Bugler*, which, if nothing else, would allow him to hone his craft while making some extra money on the side. Hemingway, he believed, had done something of the sort when he was a young man. But Bowles sincerely doubted whether any of the periodicals for which Hemingway had written had featured, as its front-page headline, 'New Stop Sign Installed', or a police blotter mentioning as its single instance of unlawfulness the theft of a ham-and-cheese submarine sandwich, partially eaten, valued at approximately one-and-one-half pounds sterling.

In fact, Bowles could rightly credit *The Bugler* with getting him through his most difficult moments of self-doubt. There is no greater motivation than to gaze upon the consequences of failure, which is one of the reasons he read each and every edition of *The Bugler* cover to cover as soon as it arrived. Taking the newest one inside, he dropped it on the kitchen table and went over to the garbage bin to deposit Mr. Bosrum's—or possibly one of Bosrum's sons'—reply to his life's work. Something changed his mind, however, and he went instead over to the refrigerator and with a cheap, rubber magnet in the shape of the state of Hawaii, stuck the letter to the door of the freezer. With a red, felt-tip pen he wrote—directly under where it said, "Seriously?"—the words "One-hundred percent!"

'Dialoguing', it was called, an empowerment trick he had picked up from a recent issue of *Writers & Writing* magazine, intended to give back to the author a sense of control lost in the inherently anonymous nature of the submission-rejection letter dynamic. Whether or not it actually made him feel any better he couldn't say, but he at least *believed* he felt better. Which, he supposed, was pretty much the same thing.

Once he had prepared his breakfast of Pop Tarts and orange juice, Bowles took a seat at the kitchen table and spread out the newest *Bugler* to skim over the front page. This was a moment he looked forward to each week. Not only did it get him motivated to get back to his writing, but it also provided him with a momentary ego boost as concerned the quality of his work. No matter how harsh Bowles might be on himself, he had no reservations about declaring his superiority to anyone on 'Chief Editor Nigel Quill's' pathetic staff.

Bowles saw little in the newest addition to contradict this assertion. By page three he had counted no less than seven sentences ending in prepositions, fifteen misuses of the word "there" (or "their", or "they're", respectively), and one audacious reference to "former U.S. President Benjamin Franklin", who in the late eighteenth century became "the inventor of electricity". Bowles felt an odd sensation in his face, which after a moment's consideration he recognized as a smile. A rather serene, beatific smile, the type that transcends the ups and downs of day-to-day life and reveals a soul in harmony with the basic underpinnings of the cosmos. It was when he reached the 'Arts & Entertainment' section and his eye fell on a brief, Associated Press spot near the bottom of the page that his serenity vanished and a new feeling washed over him, one which took a considerably shorter period of consideration to recognize as nausea. This abrupt one-eighty had nothing to do with the quality of the piece, so much as the news it contained: Edwin Block had signed a new book deal.

"New York Times best-selling author Edwin Block," it began (those words alone were enough to raise Bowles's bile), "has just inked a lucrative one-book deal with longtime publisher LitCorp, earning him a cool $1 million advance for the rights to his novelization of Edward Gibbon's classic historical treatise, *The Decline and Fall of the Roman Empire*."

Bowles had once told himself that nothing the major publishing houses chose to do would ever shock him, but nevertheless, he was forced to reread this opening sentence three times before he could believe it was true. When he was fully convinced, he closed the paper slowly, folded it in half, and carried it outside with him onto the back porch, where he took out and lit his after-breakfast cigarette. He stood there a while, staring out over his small square of backyard, over the brown picket fence at the back of his property, towards the line of telephone poles that skirted the edge of the M-5 motorway and marked the point where the grassy fields of West Ussex gave way to rocky coastline and the North Atlantic. No thoughts filled his head; instead, Bowles concentrated on his cigarette, taking long, hard drags and noting the strange sensation as the smoke entered his air passages, traveled down his windpipe and came to rest inside his lungs—a living, swirling mass that he could feel pressing against the back of his ribcage. He noted the sharp, sour smell of the tobacco and the way it complimented the salty breeze drifting in from the sea. When the cigarette had burned itself down to the filter, he stabbed it out on the concrete patio and dropped the butt into a glass jar at the side of the door. Turning back towards the horizon and the sound of crashing waves, he exhaled one final cloud of smoke and thought a thousand existential thoughts as it dissipated in the cold, gray September dawn.

Malcolm Bowles began to cry.

It was little more than a stray tear trickling from the corner of his eye, but it stayed with him as he went back inside, gathered up the dog-eared pages of his manuscript and straightened the pile as best he could. When he had arranged it just so, he took it with him into the kitchen and over to the corner where the garbage bin waited with gaping maw. The entire way the numbers ran through his head: two to three hours each day after work; five to six hours a day on his days off; three years, one month, and eighteen days since he had first put pen to paper and scribbled down the preliminary notes for the novel that would one day take over his life, consume him body and soul. More than three years of his existence he now held in his hands, three years embodied in a stack of two-hundred-odd, badly wrinkled sheets of paper shit on by every middling editor in New York.

Once, Art had dared men to come to it, to open their minds, cultivate their intellect and raise themselves up into the rarified air where it alone existed. Now it stalked the street corners like some common whore, "accessible" to the masses. As Malcolm Bowles dropped the last three years of his life into the bin and shut the lid, he had only one wish—that one day, Edwin Block would wander into The Harpoon and Barrel, sit down and order a drink. Maybe when that day came, when Bowles could lean down and look into the eyes of a *New York Times* best-selling author, he could understand just exactly where it was he had gone wrong. Until then, not another second of his life would be wasted hammering out words on a computer. From this day forward, he had nothing but time.

The

Around that time it became fashionable to adopt the persona of a historical figure. It started when three young trendsetters from the East End traveled to Paris and dug up the corpse of deceased author Andre Gide. Grinding the bones into a fine powder, they dissolved his remains in a mixture of chamomile tea and swallowed him whole. When they returned from their overseas trip, the trio was well received. They made special appearances at parties, lecturing at length about the importance of balancing strict artistic discipline with unlimited sensual indulgence. The newspapers adored them, giving them their own two-page spread in the Community Lifestyles section of the Sunday edition. "Here is something never seen before," they told us, but anyone with half a brain knew better.

I first made their acquaintance at a mixer in the South Hills, a quiet little event sponsored by the mistress of a prominent union boss. My girlfriend, Marta, was charmed by their European ways, and several were the times she looked at me with disdain and hissed under her breath, "Why can't you be more like them?"

"It is better to be hated for what you are than loved for what you are not," said the three Gides.

Marta swooned.

She left me the following week for a young painter who had consumed a milkshake containing the femur of Pablo Picasso. He came into the frame shop where she worked, looking for a sixteen-by-twenty-four mahogany Deco to compliment his new piece, *Old Keytarist*, and swept her off her feet.

"But what about me?" I wailed. "I'm an artist..."

"You're a nobody! Whose corpse did you ever eat?"

I was devastated, and wrote a poem about it, *A Heart Defiled*, but none of the local periodicals would touch it. "Too original, kid. Who are you supposed to sound like anyway?"

I sound like me, dammit! I sound like me! Isn't that enough? No, they wanted Arthur Rimbaud. And I was only Arthur Trezeguet, local nobody. I spent my afternoons at the park, with the birds and squirrels.

Kerouac was next to be exhumed. Then came Warhol, Genet, Gericault, Kafka, Presley, Fellini, Goya, Brahms, Burroughs, Hendrix, even Jasper Johns, until it became difficult to tell just who was who or what was what. The papers called it a "Renaissance". Every week, a new sensation:

"For technical perfection, one need look no further than Dutch Baroque master Penny Axelsmith. Her new series of portraits, completed last month after ingesting Rembrandt van Rijn's lower jawbone, is sponsored by Johnson's Subaru of Wexford, and will be on display throughout January at the Mattress Factory on the North Side."

It was on a trip to the store that I first noticed I was being followed. A slight rustle in the shrubbery to my right, a protruding camera lens...it was the local news. When they realized they'd been spotted, they came pouring out from their hiding places like a herd of rats. I was surrounded on the sidewalk...left...right...every direction a camera or microphone.

"What do you want?" I asked.

"Show us your art!" they pleaded.

"My art?"

"Yes!"

"What are you talking about?"

"We want to feature you!"

They shifted their weight as they spoke, scratching at their wrists and forearms until they were red.

"You do?"

"Yes!"

"I don't know what to say." A grin spread across my face. "I haven't written anything in a long time. Well, there is this poem..."

"Read it!"

"I don't have it with me."

"Read something else!"

"There is nothing else."

"Here," said a reporter. He handed me a ballpoint pen and a tablet. "Write something new."

"Right now?"

"Yes!"

"I can't just come up with something so..."

"Just do it!"

I looked at their faces, eager and expectant. I looked around at all the cameras and then down at the tablet.

"Well...why not?"

And I began to write:

"The..."

"Perfect!" said the reporter, snatching the tablet from my hand. "*The...*" he said. "How minimalist! You must have eaten Raymond Carver!"

I tried to protest, but the clamor had grown too much to compete with:

"Read it out loud!"

"Doesn't it just roll off the tongue?"

"Incredible!"

"Revolutionary!"

"Jerry, get a tight shot!"

"Call Max, tell him we got something big!"

"You're gonna be famous, kid!"

"Famous!"

"You ever met Mick Jagger?"

"Pamela Anderson?"

"You'll love her!"

"Tits out to here!"

"Look at him!"

"Look at that smile!"

"This kid's the next Hemingway!"

"Bukowski!"

"Rod McKuen!"

"Who?"

"He was that hippie."

"Who cares? This kid is now!"

"Right now!"

"Right on!"

"Hey kid, which studio's going to make the movie?"

"I hear Tri-Star's looking!"

"Yeah kid, who do you want playing the lead character?"

"Leo?"

"Brad?"

"Who?"

"Yeah kid, who?

I suggested Mark Linn-Baker, whose turn as the irascible Cousin Larry provided the perfect counterpoint to Bronson Pinchot's smug irreverence. The choice was not a popular one, but the press was forgiving since I was young and photogenic. They chalked it up to my "refreshingly offbeat sensibilities."

The man who played 'Wolverine' in the X-Men films was cast as the lead in the Broadway production. His gender-bending capabilities were supposed to bring a whole new dimension to the role. As my text was only one word, I wasn't sure it was possible to invoke gender at all, but they assured me he was up to it. I went to see him opening night at the Ambassador and was impressed by the performance. His delivery of the word 'the' went up slightly at the end, posing it as more of a question than the answer I had intended it to be.

The following week I appeared on the cover of *Art?* magazine, a small, underground publication put out by Storm the Gulag Press, part of the 'independent' wing of AOL-Time Warner's literary division. My new novel, *The Sun Also Sets*, was getting rave reviews, despite the fact it had yet to be published. When the announcement came that I had been nominated for a Pulitzer Prize, I received congratulatory calls and emails from all over the world, including the President of the United States, and a dinner invitation from former Pittsburgh Steelers wideout, Louis Lipps.

When Marta heard of my success, she became jealous. She appeared on my doorstep one afternoon to plead for forgiveness, but my agent Bertrand had already acquired for me a mistress, a lithe Canadian hand model named

Mystique, and so reconciliation was impossible. I loosed my attack dogs, and Marta was able to vacate the premises with only minor injuries.

Lounging around my twelve-acre pool, living off the fruits of my labor, I began to wonder whether I hadn't lost something in the process. Had my innocence been sacrificed? Had my raw potential been polished and diluted by the Hollywood media machine? Luckily the Quaaludes kicked in before I could answer. As I felt the gentle caress of illicit narcotics lulling me to sleep, the bottle of Old Jasper's plum wine I had been guzzling slipped from my fingers and sank to its watery grave. Would I, one day, experience a similar fall? On a nearby table, my Pink Pearl endorsement contract flapped in the wind. I chose to interpret the sound as a metaphor for Hope and surrendered myself to darkness.

Randall DeVallance is the author of the short novel, *Dive* (2004), and the short-story collection, *Sketches of Invalids* (2007). A native of Pittsburgh, Pa., DeVallance once served with the Peace Corps in Bulgaria. He now lives in Astoria, New York.